I0741409

AFTERWORD, by David Markson
a book by [name of author]

The 65th book in Inside the Castle's expanded field of literature. Designed by John Trefry and typeset in Century Gothic, a digital typeface modeled on Futura that was never cut into metal type. Of note is that Century Gothic uses 30% less ink than other analogous geometric sans-serifs, like Arial. Do we think the printer is going to pass on their savings to us? Of course not.

www. insidethecastle.org

Lawrence, Kansas

AFTERWORD
BY DAVID MARKSON

A BOOK BY [NAME OF AUTHOR]

A one-word inquiry Reader discovers on a notesheet, its meaning now lost to him completely: *Dead?*

In *The Tempest*, there are four characters who are wrongly believed dead, leading to astonished encounters in the latter Acts.

In *The Comedy of Errors*, there are six.

Too much of a good thing? Writer began to worry when he started filling shoeboxes with notecards for #2.

Chronicles. Being the last book of the Hebrew Bible.

Tradi-*tion*!

& the Individual Talent

(Here Comes Everybody.)

Beethoven's Tenth. Brahms' First was spoken of as.

Ville-Evrard. Antonin Artaud died in. August of 1939. According to Antonin Artaud later that same year.

Northanger Abbey. 2666. The Master & Margarita. A Confederacy of Dunces. Austerlitz. The Aeneid. Billy Budd. The Canterbury Tales. The First Man. Delta of Venus. The Original of Laura. The Will to Power. A Defence of Poetry. A Moveable Feast. All published posthumously.

Housman published a volume entitled *Last Poems* in 1922.
And lived until 1936.

Cotard's Syndrome. A condition in which one believes oneself dead. Named for the neurologist Proust based his Professor Cottard on.

AFTERWORD, BY DAVID MARKSON, a book by [name of author]

One takeaway from *A Moveable Feast* is that Ezra Pound was a generous and faithful friend. No mention of whether he was for or against the extermination of the Jews.

Reviewers that protest that Novelist has lately appeared to be writing the same book over and over.

What are you doing, Dave? HAL 9000 wanted to know.

All men who repeat a line from Shakespeare are William Shakespeare. Borges insisted.

The Consul, Geoffrey Firmin. Protagonist of the novel *In the Valley of the Shadow of Death*. Which Sigbjørn Wilderness–narrator of Malcolm Lowry's posthumous *Dark as the Grave Wherein My Friend is Laid*– contemplates having written.

Sigbjørn being a thinly veiled version of Lowry himself reexamining the Lowry who wrote the thinly veiled version of himself for *Under the Volcano*.

> *You say I am repeating*
> *Something I have said before. I*
> *shall say it again.*

Ezra Pound was Yeats' best man.

Proust was Henri Bergson's.

A rose is a rose is a rose.

Pythagoras once asked someone to stop striking a puppy because he recognized the voice of a dead friend in its yelping.

Greenwich Village. Novelist died in. June 4, 2010.

What a maze of complicated suffering and interrelated nonsense everything is. Sigbjørn's wife, Primrose, remarks in *Dark as the Grave Wherein My Friend is Laid.*

> *There is one story and one story only*

The romantic disease. Wyatt calls "originality" in *The Recognitions.*

> A very pretty poem, Mr. Pope. But you must not call it Homer.

Ithaca. Birthplace of David Foster Wallace.

Maiden name?
Shakespear.
Ezra Pound's fiancé would have answered the clerk filling out the marriage license.

The Rubáiyát of Omar Khayyám.

Proust got off watching rats fight.

> And here comes the neurotic titter again.

Primrose Wilderness. Being a character name one doubts even Dickens could offer up with a straight face.

You make good use of the name…Your own name is strange enough. I suppose it explains your fantastical humour. John Eglington remarks to Stephen Dedalus.

Contrary to trending theories, the Earth is not flat. Though it seems the universe *is.*

AFTERWORD, BY DAVID MARKSON, a book by [name of author]

What do you make of that, Watson?

Blazes Boylan.

Brahms' *Variations and Fugue on a Theme by Handel, Op. 24.*

> *Admittedly I err by undertaking*
> *This in its present form*

Having been James Merrill's opening concession for *The Changing Light at Sandover*.

Author, for the record, would not need a supernatural rationale for asking someone to stop *striking a puppy*.

Caden Cotard. Played by Philip Seymour Hoffman in Charlie Kaufman's *Synecdoche, New York*.

1939-1943. The deceased Artaud composed posthumous spells written in blood and ink.

Reports of the death of the author have been greatly exaggerated.

La Chanson de Roland

Mark Twain had a cat named Bambino. (Babe Ruth born four years after the author was–accurately– reported dead. So *no*.)

Wittgenstein eating powdered eggs every day of his adult life.

Too much of a good thing? Author can't help but go on wondering.

The road of excess leads to the palace of wisdom.

Pronounced the best man at *The Marriage of Heaven and Hell*.

Being *de trop* in the world. Wittgenstein "had a hint of". According to David Pinsent.

For long stretches, Hans Wittgenstein would pretend his little brother Ludwig did not exist, which drove the latter to distraction.

April 1, 2020. Inspired by a publisher's April Fool's Day gag about a lost (found) Herman Melville manuscript, Author got the shoeboxes out of storage, dusted off the old Olympia portable and began work on his next book.

Why not? That's why.

The Wings of the Dove, *The Ambassadors*, and *The Golden Bowl* were not written by Henry James. They were spoken by him. Someone else typed them out.

The *Chronicles* narrative begins with Adam, Seth, and Enosh, tracing the genealogy to the first Kingdom of Israel.

Of what is past, or passing, or to come.

Perhaps William Gaddis is not B. Traven after all, or J.D. Salinger, Ambrose Bierce, or Thomas Pynchon. Perhaps he is me. William Gass hypothesizes in his introduction to *The Recognitions*.

I'm in words, made of words, others' words. Narrator of *The Unnamable* comes to understand.

Greenwich Village. Philip Seymour Hoffman also died in. A few years after Novelist.

AFTERWORD, BY DAVID MARKSON, a book by [name of author]

Little Cousins, Called back, Emily.

Intercessor: Widow Camus. *To you who will never be able to read this book.*

The dead I love. Being who John Berryman (*né* John Smith Jr.) said he wrote for.

"For some reason I made a rather important character of mine live in that blasted tower over there. And…one of the most important scenes in the book takes place in it," Sigbjørn said, "a scene where my hero has to choose, to put it rather stupidly, between life and death…And now I'm living in the thing myself."

In the beginning, sometimes I left messages in the street.

The year before he died, Novelist received a fan letter from an author (whose name escapes), reminiscent of the letter Novelist had written to Malcolm Lowry, more or less asking him to be his father.

Amused or flattered or compelled to pity (said letter had the air of an ironized suicide note) or concerned with his own fast approaching posterity, Novelist responded with some lines to [name of author] on one of his trademark postcards. Were it years ago, he would have written more, Novelist assured him, but was now *old tired sick alone broke*.

      He was my one and only master. Cezanne! It was the same with all of us–he was like our father. Picasso proclaimed.

Harold Bloom. Sigmund Freud. Nathaniel Hawthorne.

Dmitri Karamazov.

      Undesirable originality. Beethoven's *Eroica* was once condemned for.

Dmitri's dream of crossing the steppes on a winter's day.

Gogol's *Overcoat*.

Some exposition unavoidable.

Kinship. Lévi-Strauss had made a thorough investigation of.

Alyosha Karamazov. Named for the author's son who had died of an epileptic seizure.

AFTERWORD, BY DAVID MARKSON, a book by [name of author]

Hamnet Shakespeare (1585-1596).

Octavio Paz wrote the play *La hija de Rappaccini* in 1956, adapting it from the Nathaniel Hawthorne story. He combined Hawthorne's story with sources from the Indian poet Vishakadatta and influences from Japanese Noh theatre, Spanish *autos sacramentales*, and the poetry of William Butler Yeats.

Patrilineage in the Bard's chef d'oeuvre. Discussed at length in Joyce's *Ulysses*.

Rudy Bloom lived for 11 days.

Better luck next time.

Stephen Dedalus.

A portable fatherland, Heine called the Torah.

Novelist's correspondent came off as a lost member of our tribe (people of the book), and so Novelist dropped him some lines he hoped might buoy [name of author] in that slough of despond each person of the book has at one time wallowed in.

Some lines have been known to work wonders with such persons.

Conrad Aiken having responded to the same sort of letter from Malcolm Lowry.

Of the 33 Shakespeare characters believed dead only to return later in the play, only one has actually died.

The corpse of Thaisa, wife of Pericles Prince of Tyre, is revived with little to no explanation in the least believable of a bevy of unbelievable plot twists. Many of which can nonetheless bring Author to tears.

A sincere belief that anything is so, will make it so. William Blake asserted.

Imogen (crossdressed as 'Fidele') who appears to be dead (by dint of a Juliet drug), and the headless corpse of her love, Posthumus (which is actually Clotus in Posthumus' clothes) are laid together by Imogen's brothers (who do not know they are her brothers and sons of Cymbeline) in a tableau reminiscent of Romeo & Juliet.

Coleridge coined "suspension of disbelief" in 1817.

George Crabbe. John Keats. Robert Southey. Thomas De Quincey. Francis Thompson. Edgar Allan Poe. Charles Baudelaire. Elizabeth Barret Browning. Charles Dickens. George Eliot.

The Opioid Epidemic.

Knock knock.

Who's there?

The person from Porlock.

> If you value my work, please, do not knock. Requested a notice on Herman Hesse's door in Ticino.

AFTERWORD, BY DAVID MARKSON, a book by [name of author]

Xanadu having been an actual location in Inner Mongolia.

Enchanted helmet of the Moorish king. Quixote believed the barber's basin to be.

I *am* real! said Alice, and began to cry.

The Return of the Native.

Miss Doll, Go Home.

It's so nice to have you back where you belong

Argos dropping his ears and wagging his tail.

The Recongnitions. Misspelled on the back of William Gaddis' headstone in Sag Harbor.

Yeats' wife, Georgiana Hyde-Lees, was a spiritual medium.

September of 1922: I publish these poems, few though they are, because it is not likely that I shall ever be impelled to write much more. Housman wrote in his introduction to *Last Poems*.

Also published in 1922: *The Wasteland, Ulysses* and *Tractatus Logico-Philosophicus*.

Jacinto Benavente winning the Nobel Prize and Booth Tarkington the Pulitzer that year. The latter considered the "most significant contemporary author" by American booksellers at the time.

T.S. Eliot was an avid reader of detective stories.

As were Joyce and Wittgenstein.

Entertainments. Writer considered them. Having written a few himself.

Knowing what comes next in Shakespeare. And still, when it comes.

AFTERWORD, BY DAVID MARKSON, a book by [name of author]

Or is that why?

Oedipus Rex. A manual for situation comedy.

Song of Myself

The Making of Americans.

> ...until you know what is more than enough

I would prefer not to.

> You can actually draw so beautifully. Why do you spend your time making all these queer things?
> Picasso: That's why.

The Book of Ezra. From the author who brought you *Chronicles.*

> *But Sordello? And my Sordello?*

Close friend and unrequited love of his life, Moses Jackson, was dying when Housman composed those *Last Poems.*

The love affair of David Jackson and James Merrill. Which lasted more than four decades.

As Time Goes By.

Hegel.

News that stays news. Pound called literature.

...the point, however, is to change it

Also in 1922, Claude McKay travels to Moscow to meet Lenin and Trotsky and represent the American

Workers Party at the congress of the *Third International*.

America I feel sentimental about the Wobblies.

The repetition of the same majestic ruin.

Like their grandly perspicacious uncles–who groused that Monet had done those damnable water lilies nine dozen times already also.

Though in fact this follow-up having been conceived years ago, notecards compiling in Author's posthumous mind for about a decade. The publisher's gag having galvanized this unlikely, presumptuous and perhaps transgressive return of the Novelist.

An escape from repetition. Wallace Stevens' pipe dream.

HER "Last Poems"– begins a poem by Emily Dickinson. About Elizabeth Barrett Browning.

No doubt straining one's suspension of disbelief like those Shakespeare comedies in which a corpse washed ashore is miraculously revived or the effigy of the beloved begins to move and breathe or the presumed-dead daughter brought to the prince by reformed pirates to cheer him in his despair…is suddenly *there*. Before him again. *Is* again.

Born of the all too human desire to regain what's irrevocably lost and relive the relation in real time. If only once more.

AFTERWORD, BY DAVID MARKSON, a book by [name of author]

I have discovered I can do anything with language I want. Joyce boasted.

Accept the illusion. Being the opening line of Novelist's first "serious" novel.

Come back to me, Yvonne, if only for a day...

Moses John Jackson (1858-1923).

James Merrill believed in reincarnation.

DO NOT OVERLOOK OUR EVERPRESENT REPRESENTATIVES

Hey! Stop striking that puppy! The fuck is wrong with you? Author would say something like. Regardless of who the puppy might have been in a previous life.

Le Temps retrouvé

Transgressive, is it?

Author doesn't give a damn. This being whatever the hell he says it is.

The only sin is the sin of being born. Samuel Beckett had informed a Vogue correspondent.

Intellectual property. Being an infelicitous–not to say *absurd*–claim from Author's point of view.

Possession: A Romance

Molloy forgiving his mother because she "did what she could not to have me"

The word *plagiarism*–from the Latin for

kidnapping.

Indulgences. Pope Leo X had been the first to offer from the Catholic Church. At a price.

Author freely admitting he writes for Author. (Such self-indulgence being integral to the impersonation.) In case this has not, over the years, become abundantly clear. As does Reader read for Reader. Yet we are keenly aware of each other's existence. The way Spinoza would have been aware of Rembrandt and vice-versa, despite never having met.

AFTERWORD, BY DAVID MARKSON, a book by [name of author]

No indication Lazarus needed nor even wanted to return. It was Martha and Mary who were in need. It is the living who are left wanting, needing.

Yearning for an impossible reacquaintance with Sappho, Sei Shōnagon, Cervantes, Austen, Melville, Poe, Lorca, et al.

Quoth the Raven, "Nevermore."

Post another letter to the world, Emily Dickinson! Reenter where you'd exited, Molière! Thaw from your cryogenic *Ice*, Anna Kavan! Another verse, Rainer Maria Rilke! More of those damnable water lilies, Monet! Encore, Billie Holiday, *encore*!

No. It is not to be, alas.

Why not? That's why.

AFTERWORD, BY DAVID MARKSON, a book by [name of author]

Rutherford, New Jersey. William Carlos Williams was born in. Summer of 1883.

Rutherford, New Jersey. William Carlos Williams died in. Spring of 1963.

Spring and All

Spring and Fall

Walter Cronkite removing his glasses and absorbing the news on air. *At 1 p.m. Central Standard Time.*

Martin Luther King. Medgar Evers. Robert Kennedy. Malcolm X.

American Pastoral.

Paterson. Carole Maso was born in.

No ideas but in things.

I refute it *thus.*

Dr. Johnson not having been a doctor of anything. The degree conferred upon him honorary.

William Williams M.D.

Geeze, Doc, I guess it's all right
but what the hell does it mean?

Marguerite Duras used the money from writing *Hiroshima Mon Amour* to pay for Georges Bataille's medical care during the last months of his life.

Van Gogh suffered from vertigo, attributed to his habit of nibbling paint off his brushes.

AFTERWORD, BY DAVID MARKSON, a book by [name of author]

Bright's Disease. Emily Dickinson had died of.

While at Amherst, James Merrill wrote his thesis on Proust.

> A SCRIBE SITS BY YOU CONSTANTLY
> THESE DAYS
> DOING WHAT HE MUST TO INTERWEAVE
> YOUR LINES WITH MEANINGS YOU
> CANNOT CONCEIVE
> Parts of this, in other words–a rotten
> Thing to insinuate–have been
> ghostwritten?

Sebastian lost at sea and presumed drowned.

> Dr. Franz Kafka, the gravestone names him.
> Apropos of his Doctor of Laws degree.

I kept holding the top of his head down, to keep the brains in. Jacqueline Kennedy recalled.

Now it's on to Chicago and let's win there!

The House of Atreus.

Nietzsche was said to have literally jumped for joy when he learned of the mass deaths resulting from the eruption of Krakatoa.

Also Nietzsche: weeping as he intervenes on behalf of a beaten horse in Turin.

The latter deemed his "madness".

Stop striking that puppy or I swear to God...

> Royalties from the work of Gerard Manley

Hopkins go to the Society of Jesus.

Dickens had a raven named Grip.

In Tennyson's tomb there are old bones and a copy of *Cymbeline*.

> ...Mister
> Paterson has gone away
> to rest and write.

Vio. And what should I do in Illyria? My brother he is in Elysium.

Quick, they're expecting us. Rimbaud's last words having been.

> *You are a rare bird, Ava Klein.*

With you the book is one thing, and the man who wrote it another. The conception of time in literature and in chronicles makes it easy for men to make such hoax cleavages. "E.D." (Edward Dahlberg) scolding Dr. Paterson.

> *What about all this writing?*

In May of 1968, Maurice Blanchot emerged from a 15 year reclusion to support the student protests.

> Nothing odd will do long; *Tristram Shandy* did not last. Said "Doctor" Johnson.

Redheads. The Pre-Raphaelites had a thing for.

The sadness will last forever.

Arthur Henry Hallam (1811-1833).

AFTERWORD, BY DAVID MARKSON, a book by [name of author]

Carson McCullers having written the same sort of
letter to Henry Miller.

> *My thoughts turn back to you like tired*
> *music in a tired brain*
> *Seeking solution in the worn refrain*
>   Conrad Aiken had written.

To whom? Author would like to know.

For half a century, Author had made these marks on the page and is now no more than.

Wondering just how much that might be. Author is.

I am in Paris. (Nobody knows I'm here.) Ingeborg Bachmann informs Paul Celan.

The sailor, presumed drowned, searching for his daughter in Casterbridge. Informed by the recently deposed Mayor Henchard that she has died. Which is a lie.

Virginia Woolf having responded to the same sort of letter from Olaf Stapledon.

A cousin and three of his four brothers committed suicide and Wittgenstein spent his entire life endeavoring avoidance of this fate.

Author wondering if the philosopher's oeuvre might be a byproduct of this endeavor.

Though Author may be projecting this modus vivendi.

I am worried about you, Ingeborg …you are not within your own heart (where I expect you to be), you are… in literature. Celan admonishes Bachmann.

Whereof one cannot speak…

after Auschwitz

Called Marina for she was born at sea and the sea was her mother's tomb (for the time being). Thaisa having died in childbirth and been thrown overboard in a coffin. And then washed ashore and then…her condition…*improved.*

AFTERWORD, BY DAVID MARKSON, a book by [name of author]

It frightens me a great deal to see you floating out into a great sea, but I mean to build a ship and bring you back home from your forlornness. Bachmann vows to Celan.

Steve Reich wanted to use a recording of Wittgenstein's voice in one of his compositions, only to discover that there weren't any.

Dante Gabriel Rossetti had a wombat named Top.

The successive works of a productive author are merely successive editions, more or less revised, of one and the same work. Opined Unamuno.

Julia. Hero. Hermione.

There is one story and one story only

Freud and the French *Symbolistes*. Conrad Aiken had been greatly influenced by.

Seeking solution in the worn refrain

...that's right, reiterate, that helps you on...(from one of Malone's interior monologue pep talks)

Pierre or the Ambiguities. By ~~Nathaniel Hawthorne~~. Herman Melville.

Readwriting. Hélène Cixous thinks of it as.

Bachmann's incessant concern for Celan's well-being.

Celan's for Bachmann's.

Sorge. Heidegger's esoteric concept of.

Spanish and English. William Carlos Williams would have spoken in his home growing up.

Paterson. Where Lou Costello and Allen Ginsberg attended public school.

   ...the classic caress of author and reader. We are one.

The kind of love I seek is a folie à deux.

Tell them I've had a wonderful life! Wittgenstein's last gambit in the language game.

Jimmy Stewart's: I'm going to go be with Gloria now.

How are you feeling, Thaisa?
Much better, thank you.

"I haven't been able to do anything since *L'Innommable.*" Beckett laments in a letter to Georges Duthuit. "It's the bottom of the barrel."

Yet still manages to do work "in little autumnal gusts".

The hermit crab trying to climb its way out of the pail. All night. In *Jacob's Room.*

(Nobody knows I'm here.)

But why in heaven's name is Author convinced that he only hours ago abruptly stopped working and went in to lie down?

AFTERWORD, BY DAVID MARKSON, a book by [name of author]

The Stranger.

The Fall.

The Plague.

      Categorically, with no politics. Having been Reader's mandate for #1.

Though in his progression through Writer and Author to Novelist–the times becoming what they were (not to say they ever *weren't*)–increasingly conscious thereof.

Dick Cheney's claim of Iraq's weapons of mass destruction program. Based on intelligence the C.I.A. exposed as bogus. To Cheney *before* he went public with the claim.

Ethics. Which scholars rarely bother about in Spinoza's *Ethics.*

On Escape (Levinas from Heidegger)

The zone of non-being. Frantz Fanon spoke of.

Blanchot helped Levinas' wife and daughter hide out in a monastery during the war and couriered correspondences between them at great personal risk.

      They are prosaic, utterly devoid of rhythm, color, feeling, or spiritual imagination. They are an architect's sketches, painful and precise draftsmanship; nothing more. Art critic John Gunther wrote of Hitler's paintings in 1936.

Walter Benjamin at the Spanish border.

AFTERWORD, BY DAVID MARKSON, a book by [name of author]

Let me know if you are going.

Neshoba County. Money, MS. Birmingham. Memphis. Ferguson. Fruitvale Station. Louisville.

I ran through the night, ran within myself. Ran.

Charlottesville. Where Rita Dove and her German husband, Fred Viebahn, are avid ballroom dancers.

And if it means civil war, then let it come. And when it does, may it be, finally, the last battle of the American Revolution. John Quincy Adams never actually said in court. That was Stephen's paraphrased spiel for the movie, *Amistad.*

Mighty white of George Washington to free his slaves. When he no longer had any use for them.

A $7.4 billion a year industry. The for-profit prison system in the U.S. is.

Nobody knows the troubles I've seen

The Troubles.

Is it about a bicycle?

The Land of Fae.

Middlemarch.

Yoknapatawpha County.

Aleppo. Marib. Kabul. Xinjiang. Darfur. Tigray. *Gaza.*

Multitudes. I, Fern van Gogh, dreaming, contained multitudes.

What's Aleppo? Libertarian presidential candidate Gary Johnson had to ask.

Complacencies of the peignoir. Vice-president of the Hartford Accident & Indemnity Insurance Company, Wallace Stevens, had contemplated.

There exists a wretchedness which must be defended to the very end, in one's work and outside it. Beckett insists in a letter to Simone de Beauvoir.

The Racial Imaginary Institute. Interdisciplinary collective founded by Claudia Rankine in 2017.

Race being more a social construct than a genetic predisposition.

Reconstruction

All that is solid melts into air, all that is holy is profaned, and man is at last compelled to face with sober senses, his real conditions of life, and his relations with his kind.

But in contentment I still feel...

Mighty white of Belgium to give Lumumba's tooth back to his family. Six decades after Belgian mercenaries dissolved his remains in acid.

At five in the afternoon

The child's bucket was half-full of rain-water; and the opal-shelled crab slowly circled round the bottom, trying with its weakly legs to climb the steep side; trying again and falling back, and trying again and again.

AFTERWORD, BY DAVID MARKSON, a book by [name of author]

Was I sleeping, while the others suffered? Am I sleeping now? Tomorrow, when I wake, or think I do, what shall I say of today? That with Estragon my friend, at this place, until the fall of night, I waited for Godot?

Reader may discern a modulation in style, tone, scope, subject matter, etc.

and yet the spirit abides

Death and the times have changed Author as they will change us all.

John Rokesmith is in fact John Harmon, the drowned man. In *Our Mutual Friend*.

To be sure, Author is not the man he was.

Nor will you, dear reader, be you, afterward. And yet may nevertheless be, if–like Author–you'll have been little to naught beyond lines of text you'd read and written–*afterward*. (If not during.)

Which of course you will have been. No use pretending you're not you for the time being. (Bad habit of yours.)

Once, in the Borghese Gallery, in Rome, I signed a mirror.

Because what might it be, pray tell, if not your life you have put into and drawn out of these lines, fellow person of the book?

mon semblable, mon frère

My beloved misguided misfortunate chaos-loving Malc–

Conrad Aiken addresses one correspondence to Lowry.

Readwriting.

AFTERWORD, BY DAVID MARKSON, a book by [name of author]

Walter Pater. Richard Rorty. Susan Sontag. Umberto
Eco. Toni Morrison.

Our Mutual Friend.

> Someone nodded hello to me on the street
> yesterday.

Karl Marx buried three of his children. He believed his poverty was a contributing factor in their deaths.

Despite Engel's patronage, he could not, at times, even afford paper to write on.

The departed children would surely have made overnight visitations for the rest of his life.

The fraught signifier, *Marx*. And/or the person his kids called Papa.

Derrida's *Specters of Marx*.

Marx on Hegel: The dialectic is standing on its head. It must be inverted, in order to discover the rational kernel within the mystical shell.

(Marks on Hegel.)

                              But you are the dream
              of dead men

(Specters of marks on.)

Mark, son! the father commands when something instructive has occurred and he is unsure whether his progeny has been paying attention.

"Be my daddy. Be my father." Novelist summarizing his letter to Malcolm Lowry in a 2007 interview.

Are you drinking 'eavy-like? Conrad Aiken inquires of his protégé (Novelist's mentor) in one correspondence.

Contrary to popular belief, "genius" is not an inherent quality of the individual, but rather an attendant

AFTERWORD, BY DAVID MARKSON, a book by [name of author]

spirit.

In My Father's house are many dwelling places

A book authored in the absence of genii. Author cannot name nor even imagine.

Haunted by. Being at the very least akin to co-authored by.

Keeper of the Ghosts

One rugby shoe and a worn copy of Moby Dick. Being what the customs official had found in Malcolm Lowry's suitcase upon the latter's arrival in New York.

The North Sea. Karl Marx's ashes were scattered in.

Mortally ill, Molière played *Le Malade Imaginaire* to roaring laughter and applause at the Théâtre du Palais-Royal on February 16, 1673.

And then collapsed onstage and was carried home to die.

A few centuries ago.

Malcolm Lowry responded to Reader's letter more or less asking him to be his father and it altered the course of Reader's life. (As had Aiken's response to Lowry's.)

That lines of text can have that effect. Can bind beings.

That a line is not a fact is not an atom is not data. But rather a living organism. Like a fungus or an earthworm.

Maybe we're fished for. Wondered again and again in *The Recognitions*.

Utrillo's father may have been Renoir. Or Degas. Utrillo's mom wasn't sure.

Walt Whitman and Edgar Allan Poe. The French Symbolistes had been greatly influenced by.

My poor old bewildered explanatory protestant Malc–

Aiken addresses another to Lowry.

A writer writes for other writers. Just because they've died, those writers don't disappear.
Ann Beattie remembering Novelist shortly after he bid adieu.

     –have been ghostwritten?

"How even much more interesting than the book he had written would have been a book about his actual struggle with whatever it was he was struggling with, if only his own material." Sigbjørn Wilderness speculates in Lowry's *Dark as the Grave*

AFTERWORD, BY DAVID MARKSON, a book by [name of author]

Wherein My Friend is Laid.

> There's Springer, sauntering through the
> wilderness of this world.

February 15, 1564. Galileo is born.

On his writing desk, Ibsen kept a scorpion under a
glass he'd feed bits of melon to.

February 18, 1564. Michelangelo dies.

> And here comes the neurotic titter again.

Picasso's goat, Esmerelda, slept in the hallway so
guests getting up to pee in the middle of the night
had to watch their step.

Elizabeth Barrett Browning. Having been one of Poe's
influences.

Hegel. Had been one of Whitman's.

> *Others will enter the gates of the ferry and
> cross from shore to shore…*

Joe Christmas.

Milkman Dead.

…the disappearing men who were my friends. Carole
Maso dedicates *Mother and Child* to. Novelist cited
as one such.

No longer being in the world is a being. Heidegger
had surmised.

Everything will remind me of something now. James

Merrill realizes in his Proustian memory poem, *Lost in Translation*. Originating three decades earlier at Amherst.

> OUR FRIENDS PRONE & COLD BUT THEY SURVIVE

Emily Dickinson having written the same sort of letter to Higginson. And years on informing him (re: his response thereto):
> *You were not aware that you saved my Life.*

The *line* is everything. Thus concludes Percival Everett's *Glyph*.

Certain writers' saloons near that Greenwich Village apartment would Protagonist have spent some of that other incarnation in?

Falstaff. Helena. Imogen.

After the death of Mallarmé, Paul Valéry wrote not a word for nearly twenty years.

It became known as "the great silence".

On or about December 1910, human character changed. Virginia Woolf reporting.

Worcester, Massachusetts. Where Charles Olson was born on December 27, 1910.

Worcester, Massachusetts. Where Elizabeth Bishop was born. Forty-three days later.

the lost generation

AFTERWORD, BY DAVID MARKSON, a book by [name of author]

David Jackson and James Merrill met at a performance of Merrill's play, *The Bait*, in May of 1953.

Maybe we're fished for.

> TOMORROW A GREAT SILENCE WILL BE
> BROKEN

"in little autumnal gusts"

The effigy of himself a puzzled Henchard sees floating down the river from the bridge he's about to jump from in *The Mayor of Casterbridge*. Which he misinterprets as a sign to go on.

Malone Dies?

Turns out that was not the last we'd hear about the dead dog thrown into the ravine after Geoffrey Firmin. Sigbjørn recalls it when a local (while touring the Mexican sites of the novel "Sigbjørn" had written) informs him of a ritual in which a dog is thrown into the water after a corpse to guide it to the other side.

> The Times of London officially listed Robert
> Graves as killed in action in 1916.
> Graves would live until 1985.

Hitoshi Igarashi. Murdered for translating *The Satanic Verses* into Japanese.

The dead I love.

> *Ferrin? Ferrin Priest? Will you be my daddy?*

Dante and George Sand. Elizabeth Barrett Browning had been greatly influenced by.

Novelist carousing with Malcolm Lowry and Dylan Thomas at the White Horse Tavern. Or with Fred Exley at The Lion's Head.

The disappearing men

Here's mud in your eye! Soldiers in the trenches of World War I were known to toast. Before taking a swig and passing the flask.

AFTERWORD, BY DAVID MARKSON, a book by [name of author]

There was something about baseball in the fan letter. Author doesn't remember what.

And mention of the sudden death of [name of author]'s biological father.

Another verse, Rainer Maria Rilke!

Reverend Gwyon.

Bruno Schulz. The orphan Lars Andemening decides his father had been. In Cynthia Ozick's *Messiah of Stockholm*.

As if you owned every syllable. Every syllable he ever put down.

Betrand Russell's godfather. John Stuart Mill had been.

Predictably, sales of *The Satanic Verses* surged after the assassination.

And death shall have no dominion

Protagonist having come upon his own name on one of the graves, with meaningless remote dates?

It appears very young at times, very old at others. The Ghost of Christmas Past does. It holds a branch of holly, symbolizing winter, while its robe is trimmed with summer flowers.

The winter garden photograph. Of a little girl who would grow up to be Roland Barthes' mother.

What did I know, what did I know…

AFTERWORD, BY DAVID MARKSON, a book by [name of author]

Point and Line. In which Thalia Field introduces bracketed material the reader's cognition must fill-in.

Barthes was not run over by a milk truck. It was a laundry van.

Charlotte Haze. Ill-fated mother of Lolita.

Roberto Bolaño once dreamt that Georges Perec was three years old and visiting his house. "I was hugging him, kissing him, saying what a sweet boy he was."

Cynthis Ozick is 95. Working on a new book.

Underwhelmed by his biological father, Ludo auditions potential upgrades. In Helen DeWitt's *The Last Samurai*.

The abandoned Carthusian monastery of Valldemossa. Where Chopin and George Sand had *lived in sin*.

The friendship of Elizabeth Bishop and Marianne Moore.

My beloved Judas-Malc–

Aiken addresses another.

I died of fever on the sands of Singapore. Melquiades murmurs to Aureliano in *One Hundred Years of Solitude*.

Journey to the West

       please come flying

Author wondering if anyone else began reading *The Egoist* thinking George Meredith had been a woman.

Maupassant having written the same sort of letter to Flaubert.

Boy George. George Alan O'Dowd called himself to obviate the obnoxious and inevitably incessant gender question. Which fans and members of the media nevertheless incessantly asked.

After John Smith Sr. shot and killed himself outside his son's window in 1926, his widow married another banker named John Berryman.

Bernardo Soares. Álvaro de Campos. Ricardo Reis.

(disambiguation)

Fernando Pessoa was an outside hitter for the BYU men's volleyball team (1995-1997).

Vosdanig Manoog Adoian, who changed his name to Arshile Gorky—and simultaneously announced that he was a nephew of the writer.
Not knowing that the other Gorky was not really named Gorky either.

Author has perhaps not thought through his motivation for writing someone else's book.

Being continued. Thus concludes Novelist's second "serious" novel.

Angels and parasites. Michel Serres had reimagined.

The Book of Nightmares. Galway Kinnell's lullaby to his children. About death.

AFTERWORD, BY DAVID MARKSON, a book by [name of author]

We are leveled in our humanity before death like a Holbein print, or a danse macabre in manuscript. According to A.V. Marraccini.

Context will usually indicate which Francis Bacon one is referring to.

Contrary to Novelist's fears, the snows of Kilimanjaro did not disappear in his lifetime.

An Abercrombie & Fitch double-barreled Boss shotgun did not, as originally reported, end the life of Ernest Hemingway.

It was a long-barreled, side-by-side pigeon gun.

2033 being the latest prediction for when they will become the snows of yesteryear.

Pushkin telling Gogol of refugees in a Moldavian city that were taking on the names of dead people to escape the law...

A light bulb appearing above a character's head to signify an idea was first used in a Betty Boop cartoon.

Goodbye My Loveds. Or *Goodbye all my loved.* Or *Goodbye my Beloveds.* Reads the suicide note of "Arshile Gorky", depending on whom you ask.

> *On the body,*
> *on the blued flesh, when it is*
> *laid out, see if you can find*
> *the one flea which is laughing.*

It will rarely, if ever, be the banker John Berryman one is referring to.

A little snow is starting to fall again...

AFTERWORD, BY DAVID MARKSON, a book by [name of author]

Colonel Higginson and Mabel Loomis Todd removed em dashes, lower-cased capitals and even reworded some of Emily Dickinson's poems.

Origin of Author's contempt for the editorial process?

You must know, I reflected a week's time to decide whether that comma was necessary! Baudelaire wrote to the editor who had deleted it.

Shaw's Henry Higgins based on?

Thomas H. Johnson restored the original poems in 1955.

It should be noted that this edition (*Barnes & Noble Classics*, 2003) arranges Dickinson's poems by theme, and regularizes her punctuation and capitalization.

with little to no explanation

"regularizes"

Oy vey.

The Iowa Writers Workshop. Underwritten by the C.I.A.

They don't stifle enough of them. Having been Flannery O'Connor's response to, *Do universities stifle authors?*

Mary Jane Fortunato wanted to "stay with craft and style" for her *New York Quarterly* interview with Galway Kinnell.

"Matters I know nothing about," Kinnell objected.

"Are you engaged? I'm on my way to Luchesi. If any

AFTERWORD, BY DAVID MARKSON, a book by [name of author]

one has a critical turn it is he."
"Luchesi cannot tell Amontillado from Sherry."

It seems to me, alas, that if you can so thoroughly dissect your children who are still to be born, you don't get horny enough actually to father them. Warned Flaubert.

Not our sort of thing. The New Yorker informed Faulkner in a rejection note.

The self-imposed discipline of mandatory daily word counts among craft-oriented, *professional* authors. Like forcing yourself to drink more so you can tell people you're an alcoholic.

I think that's a record. Dylan Thomas exclaimed. After imbibing 18 straight whiskeys at The White Horse.

If you're a real painter, you'll paint because you can't live without painting. You'll paint til you die. Diego Rivera's response to Frida Kahlo's *should I keep painting?*

Workshopping Emily Dickinson poems. Author imagines his Hell being.

I, too, dislike it.

You might as well know that I can't make any changes, in case the suggestion is made to you that I should. Beckett tells Thomas MacGreevy to tell an editor.

Em dash–because it's the width of a capital M. Not named for Emily Dickinson. But then why *Em* rather than *M* dash?

Amherst.

Paumanok.

Paterson.

Stonington. (Sandover.)

In case there was some confusion about how to pronounce the letter M?

Gloucester.

Dublin.

Key West.

Duino.

Though no angel, Reader would. For the record. Hear you if you cried out.

AFTERWORD, BY DAVID MARKSON, a book by [name of author]

Stratford-upon-Avon. La Mancha. Jena. Walden. Montmartre. Arles.

Quauhnahuac. Where *Under the Volcano* takes place.

"Write drunk. Edit sober." Hemingway had neither advocated, nor practiced.

¿*LE GUSTA ESTE JARDIN?*

When Malcolm Lowry drank Reader's aftershave.

Cassio's not quite fatal flaw.

Algernon Charles Swinburne. William Faulkner. Carson McCullers. The Fitzgeralds.
Jean Stafford. Brendan Behan. John Cheever. Paul Verlaine. Dorothy Parker.
Tennessee Williams. Jack Kerouac. Abu Nuwas. Truman Capote. Fred Exley. O. Henry.
James Joyce. Raymond Carver. Theodore Roethke.

Charles Olson was taller than Charles Barkley.

"The whole story grew out of that incident [the dead Indian]...I began it as a short story. It then occurred to me"–Sigbjorn laughed but without a great deal of humor in his voice–"that nobody had written an adequate book about drinking, upon which I was now, to say the least, a considerable authority..."

The now quite hypertrophied legend of the Lowry. Conrad Aiken refers to in a letter to his protégé.

The Fitzgeralds are coming over tonight. Author imagines Alice reminding Gertrude Stein. And imagines the evening as recreated by Edward Albee

AFTERWORD, BY DAVID MARKSON, a book by [name of author]

and/or Eugène Ionesco.

The audacity of writing someone else's autobiography to tell your own story.

Transgressive, is it?

So insistent upon free agency, suicide was virtually *de rigueur* among the Romans. And to a lesser extent, the Situationists.

I wrote much less than most people who write, but I drank much more than most people who drink. Guy Debord pointed out.

Wondering if Paul Newman was drunk in that scene in The Sting in which his character pretends to be drunk.

Who else except a writer sits around without seeing a soul all day? Take away that saloon and I'd go bonkers.

Cas.   *I have drunk but one cup tonight, and that was craftily qualified too, and behold what innovation it makes here. I am unfortunate in the infirmity, and dare not task my weakness with any more.*
Iag.   *What, man, tis a night of revels! The gallants desire it.*

Dylan Thomas' last bender at The White Horse. ("I think that's a record.") Which sent him sailing into that good night three sheets to the wind.

Hurry up please, it's time!

A few months later, [name of author] sent Novelist his debut novel, which the latter responded to with another postcard. [name of author] did not write back after that, no doubt recognizing his hero was at the end and he should stop bothering him.

...I'd much rather lie in a hot bath reading Agatha Christie and sucking sweets. Dylan Thomas admitted.

Even now, I read the "Série Noire" more readily than I do Wittgenstein. Sartre confessed.

　　　　Epitaph for a Deadbeat

The Blue Spill. An unfinished detective novel co-written by Ezra Pound.

Novelist would, however, eventually be written back. The way Conan Doyle wrote Sherlock Holmes back (because his readers had so lamented the loss).

It's cheating. You're cheating. Critics complained.

That's Entertainment!

AFTERWORD, BY DAVID MARKSON, a book by [name of author]

Thomas Wentworth Higginson was a feminist and abolitionist. Seems to have been an all-around good guy for his time and place. Bit of a dimwit, perhaps, but hindsight is 20/20. He tried to understand, which is, after all, one's utmost.

Als ich kan.

Adrienne Rich slammed Archibald MacLeish for calling Emily Dickinson "girl" in his statement: "I think we're all half in love with the dead girl."

Artemisia Gentileschi.

Willow. Willow. Willow.

Sor Juana Inés de la Cruz was reading Plato and Aristophanes, in Latin translations, at the age of 8.

Fascicles. Emily had bundled her poems into.

I'm ceded—I've stopped being Theirs—

Margaret Garner. Whose life story Toni Morrison based *Beloved* on.

A monstrous dose of reality. Susan Sontag called the 9/11 attacks.

The decapitated heads of Holofernes and John the Baptist.

First having read the book of myths

she is the Other

A biomythography. Audre Lorde called her memoirs.

AFTERWORD, BY DAVID MARKSON, a book by [name of author]

When Sappho was a living girl–
        Emily endeavors to reimagine.

Ain't I a Woman?

        ...greener than grass
        I am and dead–or almost
            I seem to be

Live merrily, little daughter-book, even if I can't and we can't; recite yourself to all who will listen; stay hopeful and wise. Joanna Russ entreated her "sci-fi" classic, *The Female Man.*

        Except the one she sang and, singing, made

The ongoing practice of addressing women in love songs as baby.

The Yellow Wallpaper

Manifesto of the 343

In the only authenticated image, she is 16. At Mount Holyoke.

        And she died singing it: that song to-night
        Will not go from my mind...

Mahmoud Darwish. Olive Moore. Willem de Kooning. Alejandra Pizarnik. Julio Cortázar.
Flannery O'Connor. Ivan Turgenev. Jean Dubuffet. Lady Jane Grey. Richard Wright.
Simone de Beauvoir. Amrit Pritam. e.e. cummings. Aphra Behn. E.M. Cioran. Osamu Dazai. Harriet Tubman. Leon Trotsky. Clarice Lispector. Dmitri Shostakovich. Chantal Akerman.
Dick Gregory. Silvina Ocampo. Jean-Michel Basquiat. Julia Kristeva. Zbigniew Herbert.
Abbas Kiarostami. Gabriela Mistral. Odilon Redon. Rachel Carson. Yukio Mishima. Lee Krasner. Antonio Porchia. Jean Sibelius. Phillis Wheatley. Nawal El Sadaawi. Clara Schumann. James Hogg. Berthe Morisot. Murasaki Shikubu. Eva Figes. Wolfgang Amadeus Mozart. Wisława Szymborska. Bob Marley. Lady Gregory. Naguib Mahfouz. Frida Kahlo. Iqbal. Shirley Jackson.
Camilo José Cela. Anna Akhmatova. Robert Walser. Rachel Ingalls. Chinua Achebe.
Hannah Arendt. Isaac Babel. Unica Zürn. Machado de Assis. Mary Cassatt. Huang Shen.
Diego Velázquez. Anna de Noailles. Mary Wollstonecraft. François Villon. Josephine Baker. Lenny Bruce. Dorothy Richardson. Gaston Bachelard. Che Guevara. Nathalie Sarraute.
Helen Keller. Aristophanes. Louise Bourgeois. Lope de Vega. Mohandas Gandhi. Agnès Varda. Empedocles. Kathy Acker. Simón Bolívar. Anna Swir. Louis Zukofsky. Tayeb Salih. Xavier de Maistre. Lucille Clifton. Arno Schmidt. Djuna Barnes. François-René de Chateaubriand.
Anne Frank. Sadegh Hedayat.

I am become a name.

That name'll never play, kid. Someone no doubt informed Georg Philipp Friedrich Freiherr von

AFTERWORD, BY DAVID MARKSON, a book by [name of author]

Hardenberg and Philippus Aureolus Theophrastus Bombastus von Hohenheim. Who went with Novalis and Paracelsus.

John Jacob Jingleheimer Schmidt.

Shakespeare. Cervantes. Borges.

His name is my name too.

Charles Marlowe. Who also narrated *Lord Jim*, *Chance* and *Youth*.

Derek Parfit. Bernard Williams. P.F. Strawson. All Souls Fellows.

the disappearing men

Kobo Abe to Stefan Zweig. Alphabetically.

> Though he died two years ago,
> Taha Muhammad Ali–
> …still wakes inside me,
> Somewhere
> I can't quite pin down.
> > Najwan Darwish attested.

Unfortunately, it was Paradise

Najwan & Mahmoud: no relation.

(Well, *some* relation.)

The friendship of Elizabeth Bishop and Thom Gunn.

The Karner blue. A butterfly Nabokov discovered and named in 1944.

Margaret Garner. An opera for which Toni Morrison wrote the libretto.

Say her name.

Rachilde. Rhys. Nin.

Don't you think *the names* are like seeds, so full of magic, of the unexplored magic? Kate inquires (*re:* Quetzalcoatl) in D.H. Lawrence's *The Plumed Serpent.*

Siddhartha Gautama. Lao Tze. Muhammad ibn Abdullah.

Zeus. Zarathustra. YHWH.

The horror, the horror.

Rumi. Hafez. Kabir.

...The last word he pronounced was–your name.

AFTERWORD, BY DAVID MARKSON, a book by [name of author]

Yvonne hesitated but he made no move towards her; she slipped quietly on to a stool beside him; they did not kiss.

"Surprise party. I've come back...my plane got in an hour ago."

Hero.   And when you lov'd, you were my other husband.
Claud. Another Hero?
Hero.   Nothing certainer.

From the age of nine until a successful operation at thirteen, Malcolm Lowry was nearly blind from ulceration of the corneas.

The Mayor of Casterbridge's only child died in infancy. Unbeknownst to him. He was mere stepfather to the child who had ostensibly returned to him 18 years later. Thinking the sailor, presumed drowned, who returns from sea had been the stepfather, but was in fact the biological father of the young woman Henchard (deposed as Mayor by then) had believed to be his flesh and blood.

And then in the end, realizing it hadn't mattered in the least whose flesh and blood she was.

> *Hélas, la chair est triste et j'ai lu tous les livres*

Shatov the cuckold in Dostoevski's *Demons*. Embracing his wife's pregnancy, despite the fact that he's clearly not the father (Marie having returned to him after a gestation-exceeding absence). Because it doesn't matter to him; he is grateful for her return and will raise the faultless child as his own. Which baffles the cynical midwife who proceeds to mercilessly ridicule him. Her malicious laughter tinged

AFTERWORD, BY DAVID MARKSON, a book by [name of author]

with a hint of dumbfounded joy at the gesture's generosity.

You've given me something to laugh at for the rest of my life. She tells Shatov in parting.

Karenin's sudden compassion for Vronsky's illegitimate child.

Aliocha Dostoevski. Whose mom said dad "sobbed and wept like a woman" after the child's fatal fit of epilepsy.

present everywhere and visible nowhere

Henry Edward Guy Marx (1849-1850).
Jenny Eveline Frances Marx (1851-1852).
Edgar Marx (1847-1855).

Done because we are too menny

     Wanhope.

Is not the world sad enough, in genuine earnest, without making a pastime of mock-sorrows? Clifford gripes when he sees Phoebe moved to tears by a book in *The House of the Seven Gables*.

Paul Auster translated Mallarmé's *For Anatole's Tomb*.

Does nobody understand? James Joyce inquired and then expired.

Shatov is shot and killed the following day.

...then what is the question?

Zora Neale Hurston's father was the mayor of

Eatonville, Florida, one of the first all black towns incorporated in the U.S. The town still holds an annual *Zora! Festival* in the author's honor.

Balzac was married at Berditchev. Chebutykin exclaims apropos of nothing. In Chekhov's *Three Sisters*.

Jack Spicer and Philip K. Dick were roommates at Berkeley.

We are continually shaped by the forces of coincidence. Paul Auster is keenly aware of.

John Hathorne, great-great-grandfather of Nathaniel Hawthorne, was a leading judge in the Salem Witch Trials. The 'w' inserted in the surname being an effort to dissociate therefrom.

From the minimal back story in Auster's *City of Glass*, we learn that Quinn's son has died.

The Unimaginable. Lin Manuel Miranda's "It's Quiet Uptown" is also known as.

More than 16,000. Children of Palestine gone but not forgotten.

In Plato's Utopia, children are taken away from their parents at birth. So that parents don't know whose children are whose. And are thus everyone's.

Being Singular Plural

There is no present or future, only the past happening over and over again—now. Tyrone tells Josie in *A Moon for the Misbegotten*.

AFTERWORD, BY DAVID MARKSON, a book by [name of author]

...Looking for what was, where it used
to be?
Had Wallace Stevens been?

The way Yvonne never more than seems to be there
an arm's length from the Consul. As if she might
disintegrate if he tried to reach out and touch her.

Emily, you wretch! None of this nonsense!
I've traveled all the way from Springfield to see you.
Come down at once.

Near and hard
to grasp
Is the God

Tendency to visualize a plump, middle-aged woman
as a slender schoolgirl at Mt. Holyoke.

half in love with the dead girl

The ten "chapters" of Galway Kinnell's *The Book of
Nightmares* are patterned after *The Duino Elegies*.

Letters to a Young Poet

When Author learned of Novelist's death.

You were not aware that you saved my
life.

Instead of taking notes at his medical lectures, Keats
drew flowers.

*Oph. I would give you some violets, but they withered
all...*

In a moment he would ask her, "Are we going to the

Lighthouse?" And she would have to say, "No: not tomorrow; your father says not." Happily, Mildred came in to fetch them, and the bustle distracted them. But he kept looking back over his shoulder as Mildred carried him out, and she was certain that he was thinking, we are not going to the Lighthouse tomorrow; and she thought, he will remember that all his life.

Four of Eugene and Lucie Duchamp's children became successful artists. And one died in infancy.

Anatole Mallarmé (1871-1879).

It's Quiet Uptown

René Magritte's mother was mentally ill.

53 of the 55 reviews panned *The Recognitions*. Which seems about the standard ratio for a great book.

                    ...but what the hell does it mean?

Zora Neale Hurston's complicated politics.

Tortured with thumbscrews. Was Artemisia Gentileschi. To verify her testimony in the rape trial.

I heard say the executioner is very good, and I have a little neck.

                    Second verse, same as the first

The unsinkable Molly Brown.

Oceanic feeling. Romain Rolland coined in a letter to Sigmund Freud.

AFTERWORD, BY DAVID MARKSON, a book by [name of author]

Drowning is not so pitiful
As the attempt to rise.

I must tell you about the character of Amherst. It is a lady whom all the people call the *Myth*. She is a sister of Mr. Dickinson, & seems to be the climax of all the family oddity. She has not been outside her house in fifteen years, except once to see a new church, when she crept out at night, & viewed it by moonlight...She dresses wholly in white, & her mind is said to be perfectly wonderful. She writes finely, but no one ever sees her. Her sister...invited me to come and sing to her mother sometime...People tell me the *myth* will hear every note–she will be near, but unseen...

Beneath the music from a farther room.

Bach. Handel. Homer. Milton. Monet. Degas. Daumier. Gone blind in less well-lighted epochs.

One symptom of Bright's Disease being impaired sight.

I must go in; the fog is rising. Emily told Lavinia before her final blackout.

I have had my vision.

Zora Neale Hurston died in a welfare home.

Henchard's valediction forbidding mourning at the end of *The Mayor of Casterbridge*.

Done? Done.

"Having only three even decent reviews [of Gatsby]." Fitzgerald complained.

Pukeworthy. Beckett called Renoir's paintings.

& that no flours be planted on my grave

Borges' blindnesses.

Blue. Sunset on Mars appears. To the nobody there.

McOndo

…a wretchedness which must be defended to the very end

The Duchamps' son, Marcel, "going beyond retinal art".

Her father had only pressed charges when the rapist refused to marry Artemisia.

she will be near, but unseen…

The man who painted her picture couldn't see what he was doing. She didn't really have an enigmatic smile, that woman. But he couldn't see what he was doing. Leonardo had eye trouble. Wyatt tells the "distinguished author" in *The Recognitions.*

Galileo also went blind. From inspecting the sun through his telescope.

Thomas Gilbert "Little Gib" Dickinson (1875-1883).

I looked up and you were gone.

AFTERWORD, BY DAVID MARKSON, a book by [name of author]

The fire at Ralph Ellison's house in Plainfield, Massachusetts which destroyed a draft of *Juneteenth*.

The years spent sifting through the ashes. (Twenty-four to be precise.)

Despite adoring public and publisher eagerly awaiting the follow up to *Invisible Man*, the refusal to publish *until*.

And then because *until* hadn't come–*not*.

AFTERWORD, BY DAVID MARKSON, a book by [name of author]

Malcolm Lowry's unfinished novel, *Dark as the Grave Wherein My Friend Is Laid* was published 13 years after his death.

A 348 page condensation of over 2,000 (unincinerated) pages Ralph Ellison had written for *Juneteenth* was published 5 years after his death.

> To publish one line of an author which he himself did not intend for publication…is a despicable act.
> Said Heine.

Beckett having had a similar opinion. Comparing the dead author's manuscripts to his widow and suggesting they should commit *sati* upon the funeral pyre.

Dream of Fair to Middling Women

During the four decades he spent writing his follow-up to *Invisible Man*, Ellison referred to it as his "novel-in-progress".

She writes finely, but no one *ever* sees her.

Ah, since that ink was wet, what days and people have passed away. The narrator of Vanity Fair reminisces.

Max Brod: I'm not sure I understand, Franz. Do you need me to show you how to light a match? Why are you asking *me* to do this?

& that no man is wished to see my dead body

A *Scatter of Salts*. James Merrill's final volume. Published a month after his death.

AFTERWORD, BY DAVID MARKSON, a book by [name of author]

TAKE UP THE CHALK & WRITE THE NAME
OF THE ONE SIN:
PAIN. PAIN GIVEN, PAIN RECEIVED.

Wondering what the Vogue correspondent's follow-
up to Beckett might have been.

Under the Volcano takes place on the Day of the Dead, 1939.

In 1936, Artaud went to Mexico where he believed there was "a sort of deep movement in favour of a return to civilisation before Cortez." He lived with the Tarahumaran people there and participated in their peyote ritual.

The Consul's unsent letter.

Yvonne's undelivered.

Going Down. Being the Lowryesque title of Novelist's first "serious" novel.

Novelist more or less writing Lowry's next novel 12 years after the latter's death.

In live readings, James Merrill was able to impersonate the narrating voices of (deceased) poet W. H. Auden and late friends Maya Deren and Maria Mitsotáki.

> LIFE AFTER LIFE I LIVE GETTING TO THE BOTTOM OF THINGS

Merrill. Being Novelist's middle name.

An *ofrenda*. Of sorts. This being.

Returning home from Mexico on the steamship *Orizaba*, Hart Crane reportedly shouted, "Goodbye, everybody!" before jumping overboard.

Or a kind of communion with the holy ghost. Which lapsed Catholic Author had refused to make as a boy. To the chagrin of his Italian immigrant

AFTERWORD, BY DAVID MARKSON, a book by [name of author]

grandparents.

The friendship of Maxim Gorky and Isaak Babel. Which helped forestall the latter's inevitable execution long enough to publish *Red Cavalry* and *Odessa Stories*.

People of the book.

Invisible *to whom?* Toni Morrison pointedly inquired of Ralph Ellison's ghost.

Ibn Khaldun. Hegel had been greatly influenced by.

Author more deliberately writing Novelist's next novel 12 years after the latter's death.

Fehrlinghetti's mother was mentally ill.

Percy Bysshe Shelley. Li Po. Paul Celan. Virginia Woolf.

> *I wish I looked before I leaped*
> *I didn't know it was so deep*
> *Been down so far I don't get wet*
> *I haven't touched the bottom yet*
>   Sang Mickey Dolenz in The
>   Monkees' Goin' Down.

Mexican Sketchbooks

Motherwell?

No. Being Author's invariable response to this well-meaning inquiry.

The Yellow Wallpaper

Meningitis. Artaud had contracted when he was

five years old. Attributed as the cause of death in 1939 and the decade he'd spend in mental asylums thereafter.

& *that no murners walk behind me at my funeral*

Sophocles. Shakespeare. Montaigne. Proust. Lispector.

Hélène Cixous considers her "contemporaries".

The individual...does not and cannot exist, in the vivid world. D.H. Lawrence insisted.

In his time in Mexico, might Artaud have had a self-portrait on his *ofrenda*?

Be yourself! Be you! Peter Falk commands Gena Rowlands to no avail in Cassavetes' *Woman Under the Influence.*

I is another.

Accounts differ on whether Hart Crane tried to catch the life preserver.

Ah, Bartelby! Ah, Humanity!

The above mentioned film especially difficult for Author to watch because his mother had been a dead ringer for Gena Rowlands at that age.

David Alfaro Siqueiros used his mother's maiden name.

As did Picasso and Lorca.

Tea party in D.H. Lawrence's *The Plumed Serpent*

AFTERWORD, BY DAVID MARKSON, a book by [name of author]

in which two people relate an account of being seriously injured after slipping on a banana peel (in response to another's orange peel incident). Something which Author had thought only happened in cartoons, but was apparently a big problem for tourists and expatriates in 1920s Mexico.

Lawrence, Lowry, Artaud, Novelist, *et al.* seeking the Rousseauian spark of "uncivilized" life in Mexico and projecting it onto the natives.

Meaning Found to be Missing. Percival Everett reporting.

And Mexico's gonna pay for it.

William Carlos Williams' mother was Puerto Rican. Of Spanish, Jewish, Dutch, French origin.

Gulf of Mexico. Gulf of Spezia. The Yangtze. The Seine.

> *Clear strains of Hymn,*
> *The River could not drown–*

The Great Ouse.

> *Dead?*

Mickey Dolenz is the last surviving Monkee.

Spanning eight volumes, Henry Darger's *The Story of the Vivian Girls, in what is Known as the Realms of the Unreal, Glandeco-Angelinnian War Storm, Caused by the Child Slave Rebellion* only spends 206 pages detailing his early life before veering off into 4,672 pages of fiction about a huge twister called "Sweetie Pie", probably based on memories of a tornado he had witnessed in 1908. According to Wikipedia.

As a child, William Blake saw a tree filled with angels.

Artaud received from a Savoyard sorcerer what he believed to be the very cane of St. Patrick.

Socrates, Freud and Gandhi heard voices.

The Origin of Consciousness in the Breakdown of the Bicameral Mind

Charles Yu was one of the writers for HBO's *Westworld*.

Oliver Sacks, Joan of Arc, and Fyodor Dostoevski hallucinated the voice of God when they heard church bells.

When Hölderlin talked to himself it was often as if in a dialogue between two extraordinarily different personalities.

& Guattari.

We owe the invention of the arts to deranged imaginations.
Said Saint-Évremond.

Rilke refused to be psychoanalyzed for fear of purging his genius. Wyatt informs Esther in *The*

AFTERWORD, BY DAVID MARKSON, a book by [name of author]

Recognitions.

Schumann insisted he was given a theme by the ghosts of Mendelssohn and Schubert.

Accept the illusion.

Quixotism. Being Unamuno's professed religion.

Let us indulge our own lunacy. Implored Chagall.

WWQD?

A brief complete reversal of the geomagnetic field, known as the Laschamp event, occurred on Earth 41,000 years ago during the last glacial period. The next reversal could happen at any moment.

"Sweetie Pie"

In one of his less balanced periods, Robert Lowell penciled in some revisions in Milton's Lycidas. And insisted he was the author of the entire poem.

the climax of all the family oddity

Better an ignis fatuus
Than no illume at all—

André Malraux. Maurice Blanchot. Antonio di Benedetto. Fyodor Dostoevsky.

Each had undergone a mock-execution.

Dostoevsky insisting that one could have no real notion of life until one has faced death.

...to know you can do better next time, unrecognizably better and that there is no next time and that it is a blessing there is not. Malone muses.

Years after first reading it, Author realizing the name Beckett had chosen is *'m alone.*

> *Nowhere*
> *is there any asking for you.*
>> Paul Celan breaking the bad news. (As translated by Blanchot.)

Heidegger was a Nazi. Full stop.

Ezra Pound. Gertrude Stein. Gabriele D'Annunzio. Luigi Pirandello. Giovanni Gentile. Knut Hamsun. Carl Schmitt. Louis-Ferdinand Celine.

> *Treblinka.*

Always already. Heidegger had been when Derrida.

...Then what is the question?

And Author surprised to recall on recent rereading that Malone is a serial killer.

Musil's Moosbrugger.

AFTERWORD, BY DAVID MARKSON, a book by [name of author]

The friendship of Paul Celan and Nelly Sachs.

> Who is the third who walks always
> beside you?
> When I count, there are only you and I
> together

A doctor once told T.S.Eliot he had the thinnest blood the man had ever examined, for which he prescribed oatmeal and spinach.

Robert James Waller said he had to keep a towel draped over his shoulder to continually dry his tears while writing *The Bridges of Madison County*.

Tsetse. Conrad Aiken nicknamed Eliot while the two were at Harvard together.

Le Malade Imaginaire

'm alone

Lebanese Modernism. Also underwritten by the C.I.A.

Wolfsheim.

"Sweetie Pie"

It is no doubt time I gave a companion to Malone.

Althusser "massaging" Hélène's neck.

The Ballad of Reading Gaol

The French Resistance.

If I had my way I'd've been a killer. Nina Simone reflected.

Young's double-slit interference experiment.

Who Knows Where the Time Goes?

Simone's cover of Sandy Denny's.

the lonely hour of the last instance never comes

1951, Molloy: Nothing, or little to be done.

1952, Estragon: Nothing to be done.

Somewhere in between being the last straw presumably.

AFTERWORD, BY DAVID MARKSON, a book by [name of author]

A Wayward Nun, Dickinson called herself.

When she was sixteen, Sor Juana Inés de la Cruz asked her mother if she could disguise herself as a male student to enter university.

A little plain woman with two smooth bands of reddish hair and a face with no good feature. Being Higginson's description.

Viola. Alonso. Perdita.

Half-cracked. The Colonel even less generously offered, early on. Yet continued the correspondence for the rest of Emily's life. And for years after her death, edited her poems. Okay, *mangled* her poems, but Author still finds his devotion endearing.

Julia in *The Two Gentlemen of Verona*. Having been the first of the Bard's 13 crossdressers.

The two daylilies she hands Higginson "in a sort of childlike way" by way of introduction.

half in love with the dead girl

Susan Hungtinton Gilbert Dickinson. Having been more Emily's than Austin's.

You are ravishing

Ham. Get thee to a nunnery.

A female Socrates. Diderot called his sister. Whose relegation to a convent is believed to be the source of his irreligious fiction.

Fra Lippo Lippi.

AFTERWORD, BY DAVID MARKSON, a book by [name of author]

The Browning Version.

…but feel always timid lest what I *write* should be badly aimed & miss that fine edge of thought which you bear. It would be so easy, I fear, to miss you. Still, you see, I try. Higginson had written her.

> *Als ich kan.*

> > –Truly no flower yet withers in your hand.
> > Hart Crane assures Emily.

Robert Lowell's thing for women who were smarter than him.

The boy playing Julia on the Elizabethan stage would have to pretend to be a boy. Which is a bit like Paul Newman *pretending* to be drunk in *The Sting*.

Disguised in a dress and carrying a gun he planned to kill a rival lover with, Hector Berlioz boarded a train to Paris. About halfway there, he got cold feet and threw himself into the Mediterranean in an unsuccessful suicide attempt.

Around 40 billion. Google will answer before you finish asking how many Earth-like "Goldilocks" planets there might be in the Universe.

Charles Darwin was a regular (if unenthusiastic) church-goer until his daughter died of tuberculosis at the age of ten. He would not enter a church for the rest of his life thereafter.

> > *For us, there is only the trying. The rest is not our business.*

Wondering why Matthew and Mark would broadcast

Christ's 11th hour disenchantment, "Why hast thou forsaken me?"

No mystery about the others' omission.

Beckett clarifying in 1953: ...nothing special to be done, nothing doable to be done...

& that no man remember me

Gary, Indiana. Where the Jackson 5 were little boys. As was Ralph Ellison for a time.

LO
VE

And a sensation even of gaps in his consciousness? As if moments have sometimes bolted past that Author has somehow managed not to be aware until they are gone?

And then a Plank in Reason, broke,
And I dropped down, and down –

Higginson still alive when the Chicago Cubs won the World Series in 1908. Though he'd likely have been a Red Sox fan (renamed from the "Americans" that year). Or even more likely, have not given a shit about baseball. (Like many of Author's readers who must lose patience with such factoids.)

Averroes. Ibn Khaldun had been greatly influenced by.

Neptune radiates more heat than it takes in. And nobody knows why.

Full disclosure? Were Matthew and Mark the most

AFTERWORD, BY DAVID MARKSON, a book by [name of author]

honest or the least bright of the chroniclers?

Vio. Do not embrace me till each circumstance
      Of place, time, fortune, do cohere, and jump,
      That I am Viola

         Come back to tell you all, I shall tell you
         all

September 1, 1967. The contractual due date for *Juneteenth*. (He had begun writing the novel in 1951.) Ellison felt he was close, but needed more time.

November 29, 1967. The fire.

January 4, 1966. First of the nearly 3,000 dates On Kawara would paint over five decades.

Henry James dictated his deathbed utterances so he could go out listening to the sound of his Remington.

      I am still feeling the typewriter, naturally. And
      hearing the keys.

Two centuries on, the greater tragedy in retrospect? That Keats, Byron, and Shelley had died young or that Coleridge and Wordsworth had grown old?

114. Members of congress in the U.S. over the age of 70.

         Things they do look awful c-c-c-cold…

Pete Townshend is 78. Roger Daltrey is 79.

Churchill's epigram on the ideologies of young and old men.

Aging Author, who grows more radicalized with each datum of knowledge and passing year, concedes the possibility that he has lost his head.

A ship record of the Santa Maria was casked and cast overboard.

A calfskin briefcase. Ellison's *Invisible Man* carried.

Author understanding not a word of the muezzin's call, which nonetheless makes him well up with tears each time he hears it.

> *...but what the hell does it mean?*

Perhaps it is Molloy wearing Malone's hat?

& her mind is said to be perfectly wonderful

When you write my epitaph you must say that I am the loneliest person who ever lived. Elizabeth Bishop instructs Robert Lowell.

> *You see I cannot see–your lifetime–*
> *I must guess–*
> *How many times it ache for me–today*
> *Confess*

She was 16. At Mount Holyoke.

Christ is calling everyone here, all my companions have answered...and I am standing alone in rebellion...Abby, Mary, Jane, and farthest of all my Vinnie have been seeking and they all believe they have found; I cant tell you what they have found, but *they* think it is something precious. I wonder if it *is*?

> *Ramon Fernandez, tell me, if you know*

AFTERWORD, BY DAVID MARKSON, a book by [name of author]

Plus the sense that Author could also not seem quite able to make his way across?
Hovering. There, did he almost seem to be?

My mind's not right.
Robert Lowell concedes in *Skunk Hour*. Which he dedicates to Bishop.

& Sensibility

It would be so easy, I fear, to miss you.

Simple Wordsworth and his childish verse, Byron called him and it.

Childe being a medieval title for a young man of noble birth who had yet to attain knighthood.

Cento. Derived from the Greek *kentrōn*, meaning "to plant slips (of trees)".

Rueful or Mournful. The Knight's Countenance, depending on the translation.

Mike Nichols and Susan Sontag were best friends during the latter's time in Chicago.

The words won't change again. Sad friend, you cannot change.
Bishop to Lowell *in memoriam*.

Some consciousness survives–right? JM asks EPHRAIM in *The Changing Light at Sandover*.

Author refuses to rule out the possibility that Andy Kaufman had faked his death and may one day reemerge.

You've given me something to laugh at for the rest of my life.

A one-word inquiry Reader discovers on a notesheet, its meaning now lost to him completely...

Most of Gogol's eleven siblings died at birth or in childhood.

Still, you see, I try.

"Sweetie Pie"

Protector. Madame Blavatsky called the oneiric, white-turbaned Hindu who would come to her aid in times of danger.

Vinnie halloos from the world of nightcaps, "Don't forget her love!"

Who knows but I am enjoying this?

Right. EPHRAIM affirms.

I am still feeling the typewriter, naturally. And hearing the keys.

AFTERWORD, BY DAVID MARKSON, a book by [name of author]

Cicero's ironic view of philosophers who preach that men should repudiate ambition–but who sign their books.

Architect of Chartres Cathedral. Unknown.

Ancient Egyptian artists. All of them. Unknown.

Author of *The Cloud of Unknowing*. Unknown.

Bysshe, everyone knew him as.

Beowulf.

Banksy.

Pull down thy vanity, I say pull down.

by Ezra Pound.

Becky Sharp's handkerchief. Which though oft-utilized in emotional outbursts, nevertheless remains dry.

What is it about Author's identity he deems undesirable? Indiscrete? Indeterminate? Irrelevant? Inane? Gauche?

The alleviations of flight from self. Narrator of *The Unnamable* contemplates.

Elizabeth Bishop's mother was mentally ill.

Robert Lowell also dedicated a poem to Caroline Blackwood, his third wife. (It is also about an animal.)

Emily's beloved Newfoundland, Carlo. Named for the dog in Jane Eyre.

AFTERWORD, BY DAVID MARKSON, a book by [name of author]

Cixous' long-distance call to her cat.

Derrida's nudity under the gaze of his.

> you are an *I*,
> you are an *Elizabeth*,
> you are one of *them*.

"My friends call me Ernie, said the Big Unshaven Man" who may or may not be Ernest Hemingway in *The Recognitions*.

A resistance to identity at the very heart of psychic life. Jacqueline Rose refers to.

Rosencrantz & Guildenstern have trouble recalling which is which in the Stoppard play.

Truth is dreams that don't come true and nobody prints your name in the paper until you die. Big Daddy informs Brick in *Cat on a Hot Tin Roof*.

The Universe has no center.

Christiaan Huygens looked through lenses ground by Spinoza.

The University of Vincennes. Where Deleuze met Guattari in the aftermath of 1968.

> *Why should I be my aunt, or me, or anyone?*

A novel without a hero. Thackeray called *Vanity Fair*.

Cubism. By ~~Georges Braque & Pablo Picasso~~. Ancient Egyptian artists.

Hélène Cixous is alive and well in Switzerland. Google has answered one of Author's daily *Dead?* inquiries before he had finished asking. In response to which Author has retroactively (delightedly) revised to present tense in previous references.

Or maybe Author assumes another's identity because he hasn't come to think of himself as anyone in particular?

> Not squatter but caretaker? Guardian of the deceased?

Chapter 1, from which, remarkably enough, nothing develops. Thus begins Musil's *Man Without Qualities*.

More like everyone in particular?

I am Prado, I am also Prado's father, I venture to say that I am also Lesseps…

(Here Comes Everybody)

> I am quite content to go down to posterity as a scissors and paste man. Said James Joyce.

Gilgamesh

The number of named individuals in the annals of our species' most illustrious and enduring civilizations: Egypt, China, Arabia, India?

> / <

The number of named individuals in a 1950 *New Yorker* article on Abstract Expressionism?

> *At times, indeed, almost ridiculous*

AFTERWORD, BY DAVID MARKSON, a book by [name of author]

Franco Zeffirelli's *Taming of the Shrew* in which Zeffirelli's name in the credits was larger than Shakespeare's.

all of bell hooks' books were handwritten

Toward a Minor Literature

Gertrude Stein and William Shakespeare. Being the only Anglophone authors Gertrude Stein deemed worthwhile.

Prix Rivarol. Andre Gide agreed to be named a committee member for the selection of. On the condition that he didn't have to read anything.

Olmec. Anasazi. Inca. Maya. Aztec.

Twitter. On which Joyce Carol Oates has a quarter of a million "followers".

The Butcher. Who can't comprehend personal pronouns (absent from his native language). In Samuel R. Delany's *Babel-17*.

...but enough about me. Malone exclaims at one point.

The cave walls at Lascaux.

Plato-Socrates.

any old pronoun will do, provided one sees through it

('m alone)

James Joyce's grandson, Henri Matisse's grandson and Prince Sadruddin Aga Khan roomed together at

Harvard.

Wampanoag. Cherokee. Choctaw. Navajo. Ohlone.

Are you–Nobody–too?

Why was so much begun and so little completed?
Lowry saw all his work as part of a vast continuum to
be called *The Voyage That Never Ends*. Douglas Day
asks and answers himself in the foreword to *Dark as
the Grave Wherein My Friend is Laid*.

How's the novel-in-progress coming, Ralph?

> *Allons! To that which is endless as it was
> beginningless...*

The Human Comedy

Aboriginal Everywhen.

When I must complete the third and/or final volume
of the *Lodge*, I sincerely wish an imitator of mine,
other than myself, would take up the burden. Jean
Paul entreated.

Nietzsche's despicable sister, Elisabeth.

> Mary kept the ashes of Bysshe's heart in a
> copy of *Adonais*.

*Lady Bracknell, I hate to seem inquisitive, but would
you kindly inform me who I am?*

Oedipus Rex. Wilde's comedies would almost
certainly have been influenced by.

You've given me something to laugh at for the rest of

**AFTERWORD, BY DAVID MARKSON, a book by [name of
author]**

my life.

H.P. Lovecraft's mother was mentally ill.

There is no such thing as a digression. Percival Everett insists.

"Mental illness" being a social construct, pathologizing abnormal behavior. A belief one who has been abused by a "mentally ill" parent and has a basic understanding of neurochemistry finds it difficult to hold.

Foucault abandoned the study of medicine because he couldn't stand the sight of blood.

To abstract means to free oneself, to become disentangled. Posited Henri Michaux.

Domineering and dictatorial. Freud's mother was described as.

Marie-Henri Beyle. Mary Ann Evans. Isidore Ducasse. Marguerite Eymery Vallette. Anita Raja. Samuel Clemens. Theodore Geisel. Helen Emily Woods. Elaine Cynthia Potter Richardson.
gloria jean watkins.

> *But you won't have my name in your book of who's who.*
> Mickey Dolenz sang.

When you outlive loved ones, they are said to be "survived by" you.

Surviving Picasso is a 1996 Merchant Ivory film.

Apropos of which, Author sketching out an arrogant

assholes of the arts passage, but realizing there are enough notecards for a whole book. A series of books.

No one remembers Shakespeare's daughter. Faulkner once told his daughter.

Kipling's burden.

> For I am all the subjects that you have,
> Which first was my own king. And here you sty me
> In this hard rock, whiles you do keep from me
> The rest o' th' island.
> > Caliban complained.

"Merchant Ivory" evoking a colonialist enterprise. Which is not altogether inappropriate.

What can one say about a poet who writes, quite tenderly, "And for what, except for you, do I feel love?" and who does not mean his wife, or his daughter, or any other person, but rather an imaginary figure?–John Serio had wondered about Wallace Stevens.

"Je vous aime!" Bezukhov exclaims "having remembered what needed to be said on these occasions".

T. Eliot backwards spells toilet.

> *a wicked pack of cards*

How many of you are there in the Four Quartets?

I wish that I might be a thinking stone. Stevens would

apparently have commanded the Genie.

The Oscar for best picture of 1996 went to the sweeping romance, *The English Patient*, based on Michael Ondaatje's novel. In it, the title character (Count Almásy) is an apolitical, dashing Mr. Darcy of the desert.

The real Count Almásy was a committed Nazi collaborator.

Thucydides accused Herodotus of making up stories to entertain people.

GENIE: I'm sorry, what?
STEVENS: You heard me.

It's still there, the cannon, outside the museum. It was made of metal cups and bowls taken from every household in the city as tax then melted down. Then later they fired the cannon at my people, comma the natives, full stop. Kip informs Almásy after the latter had objected to the former's failure to pause at Kipling's punctuation.

After Gutzon Borglum's death, his son Lincoln completed the giant faces of Mount Rushmore.

That curious conceit the Jesuits had explained to him, which described the great architectural monuments of the west as eternal objectifications and permanent memorials of the individual personalities of their creators...seemed to him not just laughable but so utterly stupid, so incomprehensible and ignorant, that these people seemed from another world entirely. Chinese Emperor Wanli contemplating emissaries from the Occident in Max Yeh's *Stolen Oranges*.

Ozymandias.

Romanticism. Modernism.

"Genius"

The West's inflated self-image.

Humankind's.

Fitzwilliam Darcy, Esquire.

It's *van*, not *von* Beethoven.

Dame Iris Murdoch.

Hathorne.

The real Paul de Man?

      Writer has gone on writing is all.

Charles Dickens and Karl Marx. Born in the same decade and developing similar *Weltanschauungen*.

Soames Forsyte. Galsworthy's *Man of Property*.

Steinbeck's Tom Joad.

Woody Guthrie's.

Bruce Springsteen's.

Rage Against the Machine's.

Intellectual property.

melts into air

55 Cancri e. An exoplanet composed, in large part, of diamonds. Likely valued at nothing at all to the Cancriens if there be any.

That a rap artist sampling David Bowie or Nat King Cole or The Rolling Stones should have to pay for the privilege.

Or an Author. Any Author. Of any other Author.

　　　Oh, dear.

Possession: A Romance

The counter-revolution of property. W.E.B. Dubois called it.

The resurrected spirit of '68 seems as impossible to Author's middle-aged self as it did inevitable to the self of his youth. Which makes the former and latter selves unutterably sad.

AFTERWORD, BY DAVID MARKSON, a book by [name of author]

We remain stalled at anxiety, guilt and impotence.
Bruno Latour lamented.

The Golden Age of Soapbox Oratory. Historians call
the decades leading up to World War I. The masses
having had little money to spend and these orations
were a form of free entertainment.

Epitaph for a Tramp

The Voyage That Never Ends

A noir *E* blanc *I* rouge *U* vert *O* bleu

The Color of Money. For which Scorsese cited *Black
Narcissus* as a major influence.

100% of the profits for Paul Newman products goes to
charity.

Peter Singer is a vegetarian.

Modigliani would sign the work of other
painters. This was so they would be able to sell
paintings that they otherwise might not have sold.

...Roderick Usher was of course none other than Poe
himself. Poe too must have known this hideous
superposition of reality. What else could he mean by
Roderick Usher's pictures, which became more and
more lifelike? Sigbjørn Wilderness muses.

Rimbaud having been a synesthete.

As were Franz Liszt, Marilyn Monroe, Jean Sibelius, and
Vladimir Nabokov.

Olivier Messiaen, Wassily Kandinsky, Duke Ellington,

and David Hockney also.

> *Green, how I want you green.*

Blue Voyage. Conrad Aiken called his "autobiographical" debut novel.

Berryman insisted he wasn't Henry from *The Dream Songs.*

"Goodbye, everybody!"

In the Valley of the Shadow of Death. By Sigbjørn Wilderness.

> *There is one story and one story only*

Dorian Gray.

Rabindranath Tagore was color-blind.

Oscar Wilde claimed to have kissed Walt Whitman on the mouth.

> *I have heard what the talkers were
> talking, the talk of the beginning and
> the end,
> But I do not talk of the beginning or the
> end.*

They published your diary, and that's how I got to know you. Indigo Girls inform Virginia Woolf.

> *What stays with you latest and
> deepest?*

What Emily's poems must have been worth to Lavinia, *afterward.*

AFTERWORD, BY DAVID MARKSON, a book by [name of author]

And would be ages hence to the rest of us.

Stay with me. Having been Henry James' valedictation.

Categorically, with no politics. Having also been Proust's approach. Prior to the Dreyfus Affair.

"Now listen, you queer, stop calling me a crypto-Nazi or I'll sock you in the goddamn face." William F. Buckley to Gore Vidal on live TV. 1968.

Vidal sneering at Buckley's reactionary misplay *cum* impotent machismo. The empty threat sounding like something a dowager would hurl at a footman.

What brought to mind being the inevitable, increasingly inevasible next generation of Nazis (dispensing with *crypto-*) Novelist would not live to see, but could easily imagine.

Orban. Putin. Duterte. Erdogan. al-Bashir. Boris. Bibi. Le Pen. Jong-un. Lukashenko. Mbasogo.

very fine people

The atrium escalator. Bloomsday, 2015.

Going Down

Josh Hawley's raised fist to the mob he'd be fleeing in a few hours.

The Invisible Hand.

He has nothing useful to say about fascism who is unwilling to mention capitalism. Horkheimer contended.

"Operation Prosperity Guardian"

"We trust you." Israeli president Isaac Herzog's inscribed above his author signature on a Gaza-

AFTERWORD, BY DAVID MARKSON, a book by [name of author]

bound bomb.

Beasts of No Nation

The Hardy tree. Being an old Ash surrounded by headstones, which the poet-novelist laid there after exhuming corpses to make way for the new railroad.

William Gaddis' father worked on Wall Street.

emancipatory knowledge

Colonel Sanders. Who appears in Haruki Murakami's *Kafka on the Shore*. And who cited business concerns in turning down George Wallace's request to be his running mate in a third party campaign for the presidency in 1968.

1968.

1917. 1848. 1831. 1789. 1775.

Time out of mind.

... crispy recipe is nothing in the world but a damn fried doughball stuck on some chicken. Colonel Sanders admitted.

Tolstoy was a vegetarian.

The Russian Army's about-face In 1917.

Why not? That's why.

Mariupol. In 2022.

Charge of the Light Brigade

Guernica

There is nothing outside the text.

...a wretchedness which must be defended to the very end

No, *you* did. Picasso reputedly responded to the Nazi officer.

> Keep hold of my arm, they must make room for us, not us for them.

When the peace established in 1802 by the Treaty of Amiens broke down in 1803, Napoleon massed his army along the English Channel. British troops were rushed to the Sussex coast, with a troop of dragoons billeted in the pub at Felpham. On Aug. 12, 1803, William Blake found one of the dragoons, named John Schofield, lounging in his garden and perhaps tipsy. Blake asked him to leave and, on his refusal, took him by the elbows and marched him down the street to the Fox Inn.

> *I must Create a System, or be enslav'd by another Man's.*

Blake saw angels. Ginsberg heard Blake.

Angels in America

The Roy Cohn playbook.

AFTERWORD, BY DAVID MARKSON, a book by [name of author]

The King Lear that Verdi always hoped to write, but didn't.

Shakespeare and Fletcher's *Cardenas*, based on Quixote. Lost.

Why can't Author tell if he is imagining that or remembering it?

Dead Souls, Part II. Byron's memoirs. Sylvia Plath's last journal. Emma Lavinia Gifford's diary. Most of Emily Dickinson's correspondences.

All of the above burned. By Gogol himself, Thomas More, Ted Hughes, Thomas Hardy and Lavinia Dickinson respectively. (Motivation varied.)

The Trial. Brod did not burn.

If you were here–and Oh that you were here, my Susie, we need not talk at all, our eyes would whisper for us, and your hand fast in mine, we would not ask for language. An erotic line from Emily's letter to Susan. Redacted by Emily's niece prior to publication.

Three Scary Stories. A children's book by Frieda Hughes. Daughter of Ted & Sylvia.

Brilliant, tortured anti-heroes. Ralph Ellison called Jude and Raskolnikov.

Come into my study, I want to say the next chapter to you. Author imagines Henry James instructing his amanuensis.

Typewriter ribbons, too, Author finds it harder and harder to locate.

AFTERWORD, BY DAVID MARKSON, a book by [name of author]

…a cult did form…made of readers whose consciousness had been altered by their encounter with this book. William Gass comparing *The Recognitions* to *Under the Volcano.*

Listen, I bought your latest book. But I quit after six pages. That's all there is, those little things?

Look up, Ludwig. It's a standing ovation.

James Joyce having written the same sort of letter to Henrik Ibsen.

Hunger. Knut Hamsun's starving artist anthem.

Old. Tired. Sick. Alone. Broke.

Starvation being the official cause of Kafka's death. His affliction having made it too painful to swallow.

Artemisia Gentileschi's son, Cristofano, died at the age of five.

Van Gogh. Monet. Vermeer. El Greco. Rembrandt. Fragonard. Kahlo. Modigliani.

The Hunger Artist

…a cult did form

Andre Malraux's father had committed suicide.

As had Leopold Bloom's.

And Thom Gunn's mother.

Truman Capote's mother also.

Why did Harper Lee never write another novel?

Novelist had wondered in 2007.

And if you don't know, now you know. Biggie Smalls informed the formerly uninformed.

Following the death of his mother, Wordsworth was separated from his sister when his father sent each to live with different relatives.

The child is the father of the man. Hickman reminds Bliss in *Juneteenth*.

He proves by algebra that Hamlet's grandson is Shakespeare's grandfather and that he himself is the ghost of his own father.

The Catcher in the Rye.

Mark David Chapman.

Imagine

The Unimaginable

Every moment reshaping the past.

Balzac had written eighty-five novels in his Comedie humaine—with *fifty* more already planned—before dying at the age of fifty-one.

James Merrill piecing together lines of the dead, letter by letter, at the ouija board with David Jackson.

Author not doubting that he had faithfully transcribed what the board spelled out (nor had steered it

AFTERWORD, BY DAVID MARKSON, a book by [name of author]

thence).

> THESE WORKS YOU UNDERSTAND? THAT
> OTHERS 'WRITE'
> (it's Eliot, he's thinking of Rimbaud)
> ARE YET ONE'S OWN

Gilbert Sorrentino's first editing assignment at Grove was *The Autobiography of Malcolm X.*

Alice B. Toklas had a falling out with her editor over the annotations of her second cookbook, *Aromas and Flavors of Past and Present.*

Fifty. Google will answer before you finish asking how many cups of coffee Balzac drank every day.

Swallow Hard. A novel by Sarah Gaddis. Daughter of William.

Oh, if you only knew how maddening it is to have in one's head quantities of phrases from great authors, which come irresistibly to one's lips when one wants to express a sincere feeling. The novelist, Edouard, laments in Gide's *The Counterfeiters.*

Gaspard Chardin, Gaspard Cranach the Elder. Gaspard Holbein, Gaspard Memling...Georges Perec's forger, Gaspard Winckler, considers himself.

...they're all there, they're crowding in on you: El Greco, Caravaggio, Memling, Antonello. Silently, untouchably, inaccessibly, they are dancing all around you...

A sack of coal. One critic called Rodin's Balzac.

Context, diacritic or pronunciation will indicate which Levi-Strauss one is referring to.

Ford Madox Ford was a nephew of Dante Gabriel Rossetti.

The closeness of Walt Whitman and his disabled brother, Eddy.

My Dear Sir,–begins Charles Dickens' fan letter to George Eliot. And ends, *If it should ever suit your convenience and inclination, to shew me the face of the man or woman who has written so charmingly, it will be a very memorable occasion to me.*

Langston Hughes was once asked by a confused waiter if he was Mexican or Negro (Hughes being mixed race). Because, the waiter remarked, he might serve the former, but not the latter.

Not Without Laughter. Hughes called his debut novel.

Pushkin's great-grandfather was an African prince.

Missouri. Where the quintessential Englishman, T.S. Eliot, was born and raised.

Ismail Noor Muhammad Abdul Rahman. Who changed his surname to Merchant and co-produced the films *Howard's End, The White Countess, Shakespeare Wallah, A Room with a View,* et al.

Fort Myers, Florida. D.H. Lawrence targeted as site for the Utopia Bertrand Russell would help him establish.

Arizona. Where London Bridge is now.

Paul Valéry was Italian. And an anti-Dreyfusard.

You mistake your imagination for truth. Russell told Lawrence.

AFTERWORD, BY DAVID MARKSON, a book by [name of author]

Some confusion unavoidable as to what's new material, Novelist, words of other authors, lore, historical facts or the problematic Novelist composed of words of others, lore or historical facts. Such confusion having been the whole point from word one.

Though Author has endeavored a textual key, if the reader is paying attention. While admitting he's not always certain which is which. And not giving a damn what the same critics who pestered Novelist about it have to say.

In Ballast to the White Sea. The manuscript of which is burned in the fire that destroyed the Wilderness home in Lowry's *Dark as the Grave Wherein My Friend is Laid.*

Based on a draft of *Under the Volcano* that had burned in a house fire. Shortly after another draft had been left behind at a bar.

Juneteenth. A condensation.

> Accustomed, or wearily acquiescent, does Reader mean?

Spinoza and Charlotte Brönte. George Eliot had been greatly influenced by.

Ethics?

> (it's Eliot, he's thinking of Rimbaud)

...for the growing good of the world...

G.E. Moore's esteem for Wittgenstein because the latter was the only person he'd ever seen look puzzled at his own lectures.

I try to stay in a constant state of confusion just because of the expression it leaves on my face. Says method actor, Johnny Depp.

The Oscar for most authentic slap goes to...Jerry Lawler for his slap of Andy Kaufman on Letterman.

Idaho. The Italian fascist Ezra Pound was born in.

QAnon is believed to be a biracial man living in the Philippines.

The untethered indexicals in the Molloy trilogy.

> *That is not what I meant at all, that is not it at all.*

If not channeling *à la* Merrill, then at least an enthusiast's reenactment. Author getting a feel for how it works. How the cards are accumulated, placed, shuffled and reshuffled. How the text is lived with.

Transcendental Meditation. The "comedian" Andy Kaufman was apparently serious about.

Louise Lawler and Cindy Sherman were part of the so-called *Pictures Generation*.

The Rothko Chapel. Deep in the heart of Texas. (*clap clap clap clap*)

"A placid life." Countee Cullen had led. According to the white guys who edited the second edition of the Norton Anthology of Modern Poetry.

AFTERWORD, BY DAVID MARKSON, a book by [name of author]

Of all the things that happened there…

Jerry Lawler's friendship with Andy Kaufman. Which the former had to conceal, remaining in character when asked about the latter's recent death on air before a wrestling match. Brushing off the question and going on about how he was going to crush his opponent.

Commitment to the bit.

Because he was he, and I was I

The pure gesture which separates good from evil. Roland Barthes on professional wrestling.

Emmett Grogan (aka Kenny Wisdom) once delivered a rousing speech at The Dialectics of Liberation Conference in 1967 which received a standing ovation. Immediately after which he revealed that the speech was one Hitler had made in 1937.

& The Unnamable

…perhaps all they have told me has reference to a single existence, the confusion of identities being merely apparent and due to my inaptitude to assume any…

So I Said I Am Ezra

I must go in; the fog is rising.

Stay with me.

New Jersey. Where Penzias and Wilson tuned in to the origin of the Universe.

According to Emmett Grogan, that is. No one from the conference recalls any such speech.

This sentence is a lie.

The broken pickle dish in Ethan Frome.

Aromas and Flavors of Past and Present

dont let bygones be bygones
Emily implored.

Golden bow?
No, bowl. Golden *bowl*, with an 'l'.
Ah, got it. Go on.

Exit Through the Gift Shop

Banksy has a silver tooth.

The *pobrecitos* chasing the Consul onto that carnival ride. All his possessions flung from his pockets in the whirl.

Let everything go! Everything particularly that provided means of ingress or egress, went bond for, gave meaning or character, or purpose or identity to that frightful bloody nightmare he was forced to carry around with him everywhere upon his back, that went by the name of Geoffrey Firmin…

The truth of the path that leads to the end of suffering. Coming in at #4 on the short list of Noble Truths.

AFTERWORD, BY DAVID MARKSON, a book by [name of author]

To be or not to be. (Afterword.) That is the question.

Are you too deeply occupied to say if my verse is alive? Emily had inquired of Higginson.

>   "I just walked back in this instant. With two reams of copy paper and some ribbons." "Hey! Are you really going to get started?" "Now all I need are some words."

Adding, Should you feel it breathed—and had you leisure to tell me, I should feel quick gratitude.

Right. EPHRAIM affirms.

Vasari's *Lives.*

I'm not going to write for posterity. Said Elmore Leonard. I'm going to write to make a buck.

That's Entertainment!

>   *And hold there is no sin but ignorance.*

Willa Cather Living. Edith Lewis entitled the bio of her dearly departed domestic partner.

A booklength platitude. Is Author unabashedly leaning into?

>   I am still feeling the typewriter, naturally. And hearing the keys.

S-t-a-y…w-i-t-h…m-e.

The Dead Father.

>   *Hawthorne appals, entices–*

AFTERWORD, BY DAVID MARKSON, a book by [name of author]

Emily tells Higginson.

At the heart of each galaxy is a supermassive black hole.

Painters who weren't afraid of spaces, of…cluttering up every space with detail everything vain and separate affirming itself for fear that…for fear of leaving any space for transition, for forms to…to share each other and…in the Middle Ages when everything was in pieces and gilding the pieces, yes, to ensure their separation for fear there was no God…

I stop somewhere, waiting for you.

Luke said: Like poets, after they're dead.
Albert said: Like poets, just.
Luke said: Fucking lot of good that is, mate. I mean, when you're dead you're fucking dead, aren't you?
Albert said: No.

Germany's glory. Levinas initially dubbed Heidegger.

Sins of omission.

34 if you count Hamlet's dad.

Once, in the Borghese Gallery, in Rome, I signed a mirror.

I did that in one of the women's rooms with a lipstick.

What I was signing was an image of myself, naturally.

Should anybody else have looked, where my signature would have been was under the other person's image, however.

Doubtless I would not have signed it, had there been anybody else to look.

Though in fact the name I put down was Giotto.

Viv Eliot having been the model for Mistress Kate?

Is this me? The Consul asks his reflection in a mescaline haze.

Parmigianino's *Self-portrait in a Convex Mirror.*

Ashbery's.

Dilige et quod vis fac.

Hence the periods? (Viv's.)

Much ado about menstruation. Critics had made.

Madame Bovary, *c'est moi.*

Eliot's first wife, Vivienne, insisted upon washing her own bedsheets. Even when staying at a hotel.

Lady M.   Out, damned spot!

I am in no way certain what this is connected to either, but I suspect it is connected to more than I

AFTERWORD, BY DAVID MARKSON, a book by [name of author]

once believed it to be connected to.

Huck Finn. Nick Caraway. Charles Kinbote.

The presence of Author. To Reader.

Accept the illusion.

It was a wrong number that started it, the telephone ringing three times in the dead of the night and the voice on the other end asking for someone he was not.

It being *The New York Trilogy* and *he* being Paul Auster, who claimed to have actually received this phone call. Which Author has no good reason to doubt.

The presence of Reader. To Author.

You asked me if I wrote now?
I have no other Playmate–

But he's in doubt as to which side's in or out of the mirror. Elizabeth Bishop's Gentleman of Shalott is.

That uncanny presence which seems to abide in solitude.

(Close the book and quiet your breathing...are you entirely alone?)

Batter my heart, third person God!

Saul Bellow, John Hersey and Ralph Ellison shared a house in Key West.

The question of the authorship of *Pericles, Prince of*

Tyre. Or of all the other plays for that matter.

The question of Mikhail Sholokhov's authorship of *And Quiet Flows the Don*.

The question of Dmitri Shostakovich's authorship of his *Memoirs*.

The question of how much Margerie, Viv and Zelda had authored for Malcolm, Tom and Scott.

The question of authorship.

> They flash upon that inward eye
> Which is the bliss of solitude
> ~~William Wordsworth~~ Mary
> Wordsworth (née Hutchison)

The most prolific period of Corot's career came in the 1970s in which it is estimated that he painted over 1,200 canvases. About a century after his death.

What is the use of doing over again what other people have done already? The novelist Edouard asks himself in Gide's *The Counterfeiters*.

John Lennon was initially wary of revealing how much of his work was actually Yoko's. Sheepishly admitting as much shortly before his death.

In the basement of a D.C. pizza parlor, a cabal of democrats molest, kill and then eat babies. Claims QAnon and his followers unhesitatingly believe him. Undeterred by the revelation that the pizza parlor in question has no basement.

WWQD?

AFTERWORD, BY DAVID MARKSON, a book by [name of author]

Cuts both ways. A double-edged sword does.

It was a black flag. Being how Thomas Hardy *sentenced* Tess of the d'Urbevilles to death.

Andrew Eliot, T.S. Eliot's first American ancestor, was a member of the jury during the Salem witch trials.

Ha(w)thorne's Fanshawe.

Auster's.

Cymothoa exigua. A sea creature which enters a fish through its gills, eats its tongue and then becomes the tongue.

Rye ergot. A fungus blight that forms hallucinogenic drugs in bread. Historians believe to have been the cause of behavior deemed witchcraft, which led to the Salem Trials.

Devil's advocate. John Milton had unwittingly(?) played.

Quixote is born in the mind of Cervantes as an object of ridicule, not a heroic champion of the imagination.

January 6th.

Beethoven's 10th.

Author's 5th being a sort of greatest hits with new tracks.

How many of you are there in the quartet?

(It is you talking just as much as myself, I act as the tongue of you...)

Or a reboot.

That's Entertainment!

It rained for a million years. To make the oceans.

Oklahoma! Home to Ralph Ellison, N. Scott Momaday, Louis L'Amour, John Berryman, and Joy Harjo.

The Trail of Tears.

…to ourselves and our posterity…

It is over. Anton Webern muttered after being shot by an American soldier while smoking a cigar in the open air so as not to disturb his grandchildren after a pleasant family dinner.

William Gaddis eloped with his first wife.

Ezra Pound: *What thou lov'st well is thy true heritage.*

Even Camilla had enjoyed masquerades, of the same sort where the mask may be dropped at that critical moment it presumes itself as reality. Thus begins *The Recognitions.*

–I've really practically finished this novel, all I have to do now is put in the motivation, said a young man at the next table he stopped near.
–I've been reading Dante trying to get some ideas.

To his credit, the soldier who'd shot Webern was haunted by the homicide and drank himself to death.

Ezra Pound: *I lost my center fighting the world.*

AFTERWORD, BY DAVID MARKSON, a book by [name of author]

"I'm the wrong guy to ask about Andy Kaufman. When somebody dies you're supposed to ask somebody who, ya know, thought a lot about them....I hope when I die they don't ask Jimmy Hart about me."

Hart being Lawler's mortal enemy in the wrestling world. And also, no doubt, another of his close friends.

I have no other Playmate–

Infinite Jest being a species of infinite jest?

Springer's mistress, Jessica Cornford, modeled on Alma Mahler? While Author is at it. Because he prefers to think she wasn't based on someone married-with-children Novelist had known. In the biblical sense.

Ham. Use every man after his desert and who should 'scape whipping?

Dickens to the widows and orphans of London *vs.* Dickens to his own wife and children.

Love is not all: it is not meat nor drink

Many Nazi elites, including Hitler himself, were vegetarians.

Frothy-mouthed. TIME's review of *Mein Kampf* characterized its author's prose.

America's first paper mill was established in Philadelphia. As was the first library. And the first theatre.

Lyle Kessler's *Orphans.*

James Merrill was born in the Greenwich Village townhouse that was bombed by *The Weathermen* in 1970.

Marlowe and Kyd were roommates.

ALL, ALL ASSEMBLED JUST AS NEEDS BE FOR SUCH A GRIND OF WORK.

Walt Whitman refused to believe Shakespeare had been Shakespeare.

Your turn to rinse the chamber pot, Kit.
No it damn well is not, Tom.

…small Latin and less Greek

Derrida's son, Jean, wrote his dissertation on William of Ockham.

All this, when will all this have been…just play?

Had Novelist authored a single metaphor in the quartet?

Raymond Queneau and the chemical engineer François Le Lionnais founded *Oulipo* in 1960.

Juneteenth. The greatest novel never written.

Blind Boone's inability to replay Scott Joplin's final outpouring note for note. In Tyehimba Jess' *Olio*.

Four coats of white gesso.

'Like' and 'like' and 'like'——but what is the thing that lies beneath the semblance of the thing? Virginia Woolf wondered.

AFTERWORD, BY DAVID MARKSON, a book by [name of author]

No ideas but in things

Harlem's unofficial diplomat. Langston Hughes was known as.

Though in fact the name I put down was Giotto.

Homo Ludens

Though according to Hitler's food tester, Margot Woelk, the Führer had a fondness for game pie and received regular injections of a protein serum made from bull testicles.

God, the things men used to do.

Aromas of the Past and Present

There is laughter because there is nothing to laugh at. Adorno surmised.

When he was dying, Spinoza requested that his name not be put on the *Ethics*, saying that such affectations were unworthy of a philosopher.

According to howold.com, Lyle Kessler is 122 years old.

William Gaddis worked as a fact-checker for the *New Yorker*.

(disambiguation)

William Gaddis is a right-handed pitcher for the Hartford Yard Goats, a minor league affiliate of the Colorado Rockies.

Wallace Stevens may or may not have been baptized a Catholic on his deathbed.

After the Young British Artists show of 1937 received negative reviews, Francis Bacon destroyed all the paintings he'd shown in it.

...where by day picturesque painters infest picturesque alleys painting the same picturesque painting painted so many times before...

Alma Mahler's first kiss was with Gustav Klimt. Her first husband was Gustav Mahler. Second: Walter Gropius. Third: Franz Werfel. Lovers: numerous, illustrious.

To recipient unknown [about 1858]

Dear Master,

The Shakespeare & Company bookstore in Paris is not the one Sylvia Beach owned, but merely named in honor.

Joyce: I have discovered I can do anything with language I want.

Beckett: ...(belches, looks down at his hands)

Don't try and shit higher than your arse. Wittgenstein admonished.

How to Do Things with Words. J.L. Austin instructor.

Verlaine on "eloquence".

Bertrand Russell's parable of the chicken at the chicken run.

AFTERWORD, BY DAVID MARKSON, a book by [name of author]

Harold Bloom and Sigmund Freud theorized the desire to replace one's father.

Preparing for a move in 1966, Georges Perec put all his manuscripts into one cardboard suitcase and waste papers into another. Then mixed up the suitcases.

I've given up the office, but not the frock. I still write. What else can I do? Quoth Sartre in his bildungsroman memoir, *The Words*.

Dante fell in love with Beatrice at first sight.

She was nine years old at the time.

Petrarch's sister was seduced by a pope.

Bernard sneak-reading the diary of Edouard in which Edouard has written about sneak-reading someone else's diary. In *The Counterfeiters*.

That's right. *Nine*.

Laura de Noves of Avignon died of the plague.

Kokoschka sleeping with an effigy of Alma Mahler.

The newspaper article about an ape who when given charcoal and paper drew the bars of his cell. Which Nabokov cited as inspiration for *Lolita*.

The lugubrious axe-grindings of a monomaniacal pedophile. Would be a reductive, but not altogether unjust review of *La Commedia*.

Mickey Sabbath masturbating over his mistress's grave.

Joséphine de Beauharnais. Maud Gonne. Jeanne Duval. Gala. Lou Andreas-Salomé.

Suffering from neurosyphilis, De Maupassant became unable to recognize himself in a mirror. He would greet his reflection, bow and try to shake hands with it.

Barthes. Barth. Barthelme.

Catherine the Great once ordered that her doppelgänger be shot after it had been seen seated upon her throne.

And I only am escaped alone to tell thee

AFTERWORD, BY DAVID MARKSON, a book by [name of author]

Joseph Haydn's famous last words: *Children, be comforted. I am well.*

It is later than you know. Baudelaire had printed onto the face of his clock–after having broken off its hands.

durée

Haydn's London Symphonies. In all likelihood being performed somewhere in the world this evening, two centuries later.

> *If end I gained*
> *It ends beyond*

Hadyn. Being how his name was spelled in the first edition of the last novel. Novelist would surely have noticed and ground his teeth over.

Author is experimenting with keeping himself out of here as much as possible because? Where can the book possibly wind up without him?

Being what Author had been wondering. Before.

Has Novelist ever known many who could not contrive some way to keep the pot boiling during fallow stretches?

Poetic license would be misapprehended thereby, but Author doesn't give a damn.

This being whatever the hell he says it is. Requiring no one's corroboration.

Fearing the imminent loss of his soprano, a choirmaster asked the young Haydn if he might

AFTERWORD, BY DAVID MARKSON, a book by [name of author]

consider castration.

Ocean Vuong's mother was mentally ill.

All literature is scarry. It celebrates the wound and repeats the lesion. Dr. Hélène Cixous' diagnosis.

Parerga and Paralipomena. The latter being what the Greeks called *The Book of Chronicles*.

The show must go on. Originating in Shakespeare's Henry IV and popularized by circus entertainers of the 19th century.

> I am still feeling the typewriter, naturally. And hearing the keys.

Plutarch's *Parallel Lives*.

> *Seeking solution in the worn refrain*

Seriously?...*No*. One imagines Haydn having responded to the choirmaster.

Hemingway's mother dressed him as a girl. Resulting in one of the most epic backfires in parental history.

Avicenna. Averroes had been greatly influenced by.

Haydn's copyist Johann Radnitzky froze to death in his room one morning in January 1790, as he was copying out a score.

Hemingway once boxed a few rounds with the scrawny and decidedly unathletic Ezra Pound. And bragged about beating up Wallace Stevens when the latter was an old man (20 years Hemingway's senior).

…what more for the elderly man in the house at the cemetery…

And Reader? And Reader?

The older man folded one hand over the other, assumed a somber air before what he gathered would be an exposition of the history of the monastery, or the Order, or some such, so carefully did the young monk handle it, and found himself gazing at the large pages of a private scrapbook. One after another, the breathless owner turned the pages, slowly enough that each might be thoroughly perused. They were all pictures of typewriters.

The work will know its own reason.

Vienna. Some of *The London Symphonies* had been composed in.

The MacBeth and Othello Verdi had always hoped to compose. And then did.

O, what a number of lies this young man has told about me. Said Socrates, the first time he heard Plato read one of his dialogues.

35 if you count Banquo.

AFTERWORD, BY DAVID MARKSON, a book by [name of author]

Miguel de Cervantes Saavedra's *El ingenioso hidalgo don Quixote de la Mancha*.

Perhaps he is me.

The found manuscript framing device.

Frankenstein. Either/Or. Hero of Our Time. Narrative of Arthur Gordon Pym. Sartor Resartus. Thus Spake Zarathustra. The Turn of the Screw. Call of Cthulhu. The Sufferings of Young Werther. Pale Fire. House of Leaves. Children of the Ghetto. The Name of the Rose.

Ruth Ozeki's *Tale for the Time Being*.

Being and Time.

Being and Nothingness.

Being being a bone of contention. Then as now.

Forgive me, I've dropped into philosophy again. Vershinin apologizes for in Chekhov's *Three Sisters*.

No one dies of fatal truths nowadays: there are too many antidotes. Nietzsche observed.

> If I had to do the whole thing over
> again
> I wouldn't.
>> John Berryman (the poet), for the
>> record.

There must have been a moment, at the beginning, where we could have said no, but somehow we missed it. Rosencrantz tells Guildenstern (or vice-versa) on the scaffold.

AFTERWORD, BY DAVID MARKSON, a book by [name of author]

A very pretty poem, Mr. Pope, but you must
not call it Homer.

standing on the shoulders of giants

Alexander Pope was 4 foot 6 (137 cm).

Toulouse-Lautrec once challenged fellow artist Henri
de Groux to a duel. After the latter had criticized the
work of Van Gogh.

The Church at Auvers. Which Van Gogh had painted
without doors. A print of which hangs above Author's
bed.

> *Raggedy Ann. Raggedy Jesus.*

> (To Flo & Bill Williams:)

> It was a grand day and we missed you
> two, one and
> all missed you...

> > Best wishes and love from
> > everyone who was here,

> > Josie

Return to Paterson. Part 51 of the Abbott & Costello
Series: Abbott & Costello discuss Valentine's Day.

An entertainment. Author would have no qualms with
someone calling this.

Speak for yourself, Plato.

Jackie Coogan. The child actor in Charlie Chaplin's
The Kid who grew up to play Uncle Fester in the

Addams Family. After whom Jacques Derrida had been named.

The Works of Ossian.

You can find anything you want in the church. Except God. Van Gogh lamented.

Art in place of religion. Tenet of Romanticism and its grandchild, Modernism.

People of the book.

Call me Ishmael...

...and Heaven have mercy on us all–Presbyterians and Pagans alike–for we are all somehow dreadfully cracked about the head, and sadly need mending...

Anton Chekhov died in Germany. His coffin arrived in Moscow in a freight car–distinctly labeled Oysters.

Brazen plagiarism. Author would plead no contest to and willingly surrender any profit this undertaking will have earned him.

Seated next to him now, discarding the cigarette finally, she thought: Chance? Steven Chance? She said: "So who is it with me in this?"

Caesar's ghost would be 36.

Non omnis moriar.

Derivative?

Yes...yes. Absolutely. Count Almásy responds to

AFTERWORD, BY DAVID MARKSON, a book by [name of author]

Katharine's "Are we going to be alright?" during the sandstorm in *The English Patient*.

Her counter-response: "Yes is a comfort. *Absolutely* is not."

The Orchard Keeper. By ~~William Faulkner~~ Cormac McCarthy.

Sam Shepard's Oedipus.

Dorothea Brooke.

The friendship of Italo Svevo and James Joyce in Trieste.

...for the growing good of the world...

Widdershins. D.H. Lawrence called the trajectory of human "progress". Our species receding from lived reality until our existence is more or less disembodied.

October of 2021. Zuckerberg changes his company's name to *Meta*.

> *The Man-Moth cannot tell the rate at which he travels backward.*

The future of the Humanities. Derrida ambitiously imagines. (That there might be one.)

A sports writer for *The Denver Post*. Donna Haraway's father had been.

This is not a hypertext.

Isle of the Cross. Being the lost Melville manuscript purportedly found by Joshua Rothes of Sublunary

Editions. An absurd claim which April fooled so many because of how desperately we all wanted it to be true.

> ...And what there is to conquer
> By strength and submission, has already
>   been discovered
> Once or twice, or several times, by men
>   who one cannot hope
> To emulate–but there is no competition–
>   there is only the fight to recover
>   what has been lost
> And found and lost again and again...

Ye are not other men, but my arms and legs. Ahab informs his crew.

The friendship of Elizabeth Bishop and James Merrill.

> ...I & MINE
> RATHER RESEMBLE TALES WE WERE TOLD

Probably male. Probably a Levite. Probably from Jerusalem. Was the author of *The Book of Chronicles*.

The likelihood that Homer was more than one person.

...I venture to say that I am also Lesseps...

& The Unnamable

...there might be a hundred of us and still we'd lack the hundred and first, we'll always be short of *me*...

Gore Vidal's 12-acre estate and house, La Rodinaia, situated on a cliff high above the Mediterranean. Near where Odysseus' had heard the Sirens' call.

AFTERWORD, BY DAVID MARKSON, a book by [name of author]

I'll sock you in the goddamn face. Author cannot stop giggling about. Buckley's effete articulation and "sock".

Dead?

Memphis, Tennessee. Jeff Buckley died in. 1997. Buckley *Dead?* search suggesting that more people have inquired about Jeff than William F...

We are not makers of history. We are made by history. Martin Luther King pointed out.

Public Enemy's iconoclasm of Elvis Presley.

The King of Memphis. Jerry Lawler is known as.

Stamford, Connecticut. William F. Buckley died in. 2008.

I refused to attend his funeral. But I wrote a very nice letter explaining that I approved of it! Mark Twain on a Tammany leader's recent death.

> *Well, then I shall see thee again?*
> *Ay, at Philippi.*
> *Why, I will see thee at Philippi then.*

Brutus chatting with Caesar's ghost as if arranging to meet a buddy for drinks later.

Foxy Jackson. Kaufman chose as challenger for the *Inter-Gender Wrestling Championship* in Memphis. No doubt to relish a predominately racist mob cheering on a black woman's attempt to physically dominate a white man. Likely unbeknownst to Lawler, truth be told.

Recognitions. By Clement of Rome. Considered the first Christian novel.

> We
> really don't know, you know,
> we
> really don't know
> What
> counts.
>> Paul Celan recalls Nelly Sachs
>> informing him.

GOD'S TROMBONE. The parishioners refer to Hickman as in *Juneteenth*.

W.S. Merwin and Galway Kinnell were college roommates.

Sandover, the house in Stonington, CT where the magic happened for DJ & JM (et al.) was added to the National Register of Historic Places in 2013.

Less a religion than a syndrome. Or at best, a lifelong lark. Books having been for Author and Reader.

> OUR PRATTLE HAS NO END BEYOND
> ITSELF

Concerned the Vienna Circle had completely misread his work, Wittgenstein would read them the metaphysical love poems of Rabindranath Tagore.

Bauhaus.

Search engine. Would Protagonist have ever been persuaded to use?

> A forty-year-old Olympia portable, in fact. Not

AFTERWORD, BY DAVID MARKSON, a book by [name of author]

even electric.

Readwriting.

Get your dirty socks off my bunk, Kinnell!

Author having recently searched for Monkees and discovered three deceased. Which unexpectedly made him burst into tears.

This is our last goodbye…

Finding it odd that Jeff Buckley had died in the 20th Century.

An especially bad century for people. Being a consensus opinion.

Though the people occasionally struck back. With labor strikes.

Three strikes. Being a baseball analogy neoliberals used to sell mass incarceration and win back Reaganites at the tail end of that demoralizing century.

Drone strikes. To usher in the 21st Century. Which is shaping up to be much worse. Though not nearly as long.

1968. The year *2001: A Space Odyssey* was released.

Formerly a fortress in the Hundred Years War, the Bastille became a royal prison in 1417.

I Know Why the Caged Bird Sings

1949. *1984* was published in.

The Gulag Archipelago

HEBREWS: 13
Remember them that are in bonds, as bound with them.

Where's Waldo? Thoreau wondered aloud from his prison cell.

Simone Weil served on anarchist commando missions in The Spanish Civil War.

AFTERWORD, BY DAVID MARKSON, a book by [name of author]

When she was eight years old, Maya Angelou stopped speaking. Did not speak to anybody but her brother Bailey for five years.

Nabokov's ape. MacNiece's wolf. Rilke's panther.

The goldfinch Henchard leaves as a wedding gift for the woman he'd once thought was his daughter. Which starves in its cage.

> Leonardo bought caged birds and set them free.

Museum of Modern Art, Department of Eagles

Forty. Google will answer before you finish asking how many peacocks Flannery O'Connor kept on her property.

Legend has it that both Aeschylus and Euripides had been killed by animals.

Our species' inflated sense that we are something other than (more than) animals.

Au Hasard Balthazar.

Agamben's voice.

Molly Bloom "watching the dogs at it".

Gertrude Stein's poodle, Basket.

Atma. Having been the name of Schopenhauer's.

Maya. Bailey dubbed his sister, Marguerite.

Ignis fatuus.

Yeats co-translated the Upanishads with a Hindu swami.

Datta. Dayadhvam. Damyata.

Blake on Swedenborg.

I am a cage in search of a bird. Quoth Kafka.

Avidya. Tanha. Samsara.

And found and lost again and again...

Ruth Ozeki is a Zen Buddhist priest.

Every man is worth just so much as the things he busies himself about. By Roman Emperor Marcus Aurelius' estimation.

To him it is as if there were a thousand bars
And behind a thousand bars, no world.

Mutter, ich bin dumm.

Rudy Bloom.

Better luck next time.

Existence is suffering. Being the first and foremost Noble Truth.

AFTERWORD, BY DAVID MARKSON, a book by [name of author]

Last night, the lyric "this is not my large automobile" earwormed its way through Author's inveterate sleeplessness into the early AM. Leading him to this morning wonder (as he does from time to time) by what mode of transportation he got here.

Henry Ford was an advocate for the disabled. And a pacifist. And showed concern for his workers, uncharacteristic of industrialists of that time period.

And spread conspiracy theories vilifying the Jews.

The traffic jam in Godard's *Weekend*.

> *Dead?*

Jean-Luc Godard is also alive and well in Switzerland.

Hallelujah.

Jeff Buckley's cover of Leonard Cohen's.

Sebastian. Guiderius. Marina.

Truffaut long dead. Godard outliving him by 27 years and counting.

Herzog outliving Fassbinder by 41 years and counting.

Bertolt Brecht left Germany in 1933. Shortly after Hitler had taken power.

Los Angeles. Leonard Cohen died in. On the eve of a presidential election in the U.S., 2016.

> *Yes, there will also be singing.*

The Revolutionary Lafayette once picked up a little

boy named Walt Whitman and kissed him on the cheek.

Je faite juste un bisou! Being Rindy Sam's defense for her "crime of passion" (kissing Twombly's *Phaedrus*).

As Time Goes By

There are more stars in the Universe than grains of sand on Earth.

>*that's how the light gets in*

Zora Neale Hurston conducted ethnographic research with Margaret Mead.

Sei Shōnagon wrote *The Pillow Book* for herself.

>*Inhuman stars.*
>*But the hours are ours.*
>>Octavio Paz observed.

Elston Gunn. Piano player for the teen idol Bobby Vee. Was actually Robert Zimmerman. Who would come to be known as Bob Dylan.

Who turns 82 this year.

But because of the accelerated expansion of the universe, the light of stars in the night sky continually fades.

>Branwell–Emily–Anne–are gone like dreams–gone as Maria and Elizabeth went twenty years ago. One by one I have watched them fall asleep on my arm.
>>Said Charlotte, late along.

Not Dark Yet

Stuart, Florida. Davy Jones died in. 2012.

Mansfield, Connecticut. Peter Tork died in. 2019.

Carmel Valley, California. Mike Nesmith died in. 2021.

> *I had not thought death had undone so many.*

Lavinia, late along.

The Plague.

> Nobody comes. Nobody calls.

We tore each other apart little by little. Godard lamented after Truffaut's death.

Art pour l'art

1968.

A story should have a beginning, a middle and an end, though not necessarily in that order. Godard opined.

Mike Nesmith's mother invented liquid paper.

> Four coats of white gesso.

Stephen Hero. By James Joyce.

(disambiguation)

Left-back James Joyce made his Marine FC debut at home to Basford United in August 2018 and has

AFTERWORD, BY DAVID MARKSON, a book by [name of author]

made 56 starts plus 12 appearances as a substitute in two spells with the club, scoring a solitary (but memorable) goal against Gainsborough Trinity. According to a team press release announcing Joyce's retirement.

Rendition almost. As if Author is Horowitz playing the *notes* of Rachmaninoff.

How many of you are there in the quartet?

Or less loftily, a cover band.

Here we are now, entertain us

People tell me the *myth* will hear every note…

They had withdrawn Watt (not What, Watt) from the ineffable Watt quartet.

Rindy Sam was ordered to take a "good citizenship" class as part of her punishment.

(A Kiss is Just a Kiss)

L'Éducation sentimentale

Jeff Buckley had gone swimming, fully dressed, in Wolf River Harbor, a slackwater channel of the Mississippi River. He was last heard singing Led Zeppelin's *Whole Lotta Love* when a tugboat's wake pulled him under.

The last time someone mentioned Kate Chopin outside a classroom.

Thai. That Thaisa am I, supposed dead and drown'd.

Per.   Immortal Dian!

those damnable water lilies

Naming their band "Def Leppard" to mimic the assonant misspelling of "Led" Zeppelin. Which had actually been a pun (correct spelling of the participial form of the verb lead).

Two things are infinite. Einstein theorized. The Universe and human stupidity.

same as it ever was

Confirmation bias. Coined by Peter Wason in 1960.

The slang term "def" was added to Webster's dictionary in 1979. Def Leppard named in 1977, *so no.* (And anyway, "Leppard"?)

Plato was clear about Atlantis being a fiction and nobody believed otherwise. Until the 1800s, when catastrophist Ignatius L. Donnelly hypothesized its actual existence.

Daydream Believer. The lyrics of which Davy Jones deemed gibberish.

In Xanadu, Inner Mongolia.

Asia and America are on a collision course. In 200 million years they will form a single continent.

Knock knock.

WWQD?

Stop Making Sense

AFTERWORD, BY DAVID MARKSON, a book by [name of author]

Rock Brigade
Rock! Rock!
Rock of Ages
(Getcha) Rocks Off
Rocket
Rock On
Let's Get Rocked!
      Titles from Def Leppard's
      discography.

Wondering if band members had watched *The Flintstones* as children. Or equally possible, as adults.

GENIE: *Okay*. You're a thinking stone...second wish?
STEVENS: No thanks.

& Pécuchet

The *crystal skulls* are human skull hardstone carvings made of clear or milky white quartz, claimed to be pre-Columbian Mesoamerican artifacts by their alleged finders. They were later revealed to be forgeries manufactured in the 19th Century.

A modern Stone Age family

Though it's possible they only meant to misspell Deaf and thought (continue to think?) that Leppard was/is the correct spelling?

Where We Go One, We Go All. Proclaimed each lemming at the cliff's edge.

Yabba-dabba-doo!

Infantilized protagonist of *The Yellow Wallpaper* crawling along the walls of her cell on a loop at story's end. Having to clamber over her husband's unconscious body each lap.

Arrested development. Being a common theme in the novels of William Gaddis.

Tennessee. Where a state constitutional amendment made slavery illegal. Last Tuesday.

When all usefulness is over...begins the suicide note of Charlotte Perkins Gilman.

Rene Magritte worked as a draughtsman for a wallpaper company.

Piltdown Man. The Missing Link discovered by Charles Dawson in 1912. Revealed as a fake in 1953.

Gathering moss being a good or bad thing depending on how you read the proverb.

AFTERWORD, BY DAVID MARKSON, a book by [name of author]

How many a man has dated a new era in his life from the reading of a book? Thoreau had considered.

Tolstoy kept a portrait of Dickens on the wall in his study.

Jonathan Franzen's difficulty with the dense prose of William Gaddis. Being the standard by which such things ought to be measured. According to Jonathan Franzen.

A Virginia Woolf scholar. Ben Marcus' mom had been.

Fennimore Cooper used almost eleven hundred Shakespeare quotations as epigraphs and/or chapter headings in his thirty-plus novels.

Countee Cullen was James Baldwin's Middle School French teacher.

jamais n'abolira le hasard

The friendship of Novelist and Gilbert Sorrentino.

Dante refers to it as his *Commedia* only. It was Boccaccio who would call it *Divina*.

Geoffrey Chaucer.

Geoffrey of Monmouth.

The Arcades Project.

In Christian Bibles, *The Book of Chronicles* precedes *Ezra-Nehemiah*, the last history-oriented book of the Protestant *Old Testament*.

AFTERWORD, BY DAVID MARKSON, a book by [name of author]

last

adj.   Coming after all others in time or order; final.
adj.   Most recent; the latest.
v.   To continue in time.

The friend had confessed to him that his last book was, indeed, his last book…Gilbert Sorrentino's narrator remarks in The Abyss of Human Illusions (2009).

Avicenna read Aristotle's *Metaphysics* forty times.

The story has no end, it will continue in you, and you may pass it on. Grandpapa informs his descendent in Péter Nádas' *The End of a Family Story.*

David Foster Wallace having written the same sort of letter to Jonathan Franzen.

Dr. T.J. Eckleburg, Oculist.

Gutzon Borglum made his son, Lincoln, work with him on Mount Rushmore for several years without pay. And having squandered his fortune before the monument's completion, left Lincoln little to nothing in his will.

The show must go on.

The man for whom Lincoln was named had also been hired out as a laborer by his father. Without pay. An arguably integral and underreported factoid from the checkered history of the United States.

George W. Bush did not know the meaning of the word "commiserate". Literally.

Twenty-five years after his death, Poe's remains

were disinterred from what had been little better than a pauper's grave and reburied more formally. Walt Whitman, who made the journey from Camden to Baltimore, in spite of being disabled from a recent stroke, was the only literary figure to appear at the ceremony.

Solitary the thrush

(but memorable)

to purify the language of the tribe

"...in order to fight and win the [Iraq] war, it requires an expenditure of money *commiserate* to keeping a promise with our troops..."

Karl Marx regularly read Shakespeare aloud to his young children.

Better luck next time.

Parmenides. Aristotle had been greatly influenced by.

Nothing lasts long enough. You want to say to each moment; stay. Stay. Virginia Woolf lamented.

Also George W. Bush: *We must all hear the universal call to like your neighbor just like you like to be liked yourself.*

One novelty Author has introduced is white space breaks between passages–thus designating them as such (if only to capitalize on opening/closing lines). Author having invented what he will call "chapters" or alternatively "stanzas" for present purposes.

David Foster Wallace tried to join the Catholic

AFTERWORD, BY DAVID MARKSON, a book by [name of author]

church. Twice.

And in short, I was afraid.

People of the book. A denomination appropriated for present purposes.

David's dancing at a Baptist church–a moving image of which concludes the biopic *The End of the Tour*–was, however, a lie to cover his 12-step attendance.

Where have all the male rock star authors gone? Joyce Carol Oates laments.

Good riddance! Originally uttered by Patroclus in Troilus & Cressida.

Teddy Roosevelt's giant face (chosen over Susan B. Anthony's) because Gutzon Borglum was a big fan. Had it been a project of the 1840s led by an expansionist sculptor, could just as easily have had James T. Polk up there for the ages.

Fifty million dollars. Nabokov's net worth at the time of his death in 1977.

(disambiguation)

Nabokov was the NHL rookie of the year in 2001.

The St. Louis Blues. Daddy Hickman strikes up out of instinct when a fight breaks out at the church in *Juneteenth*, "...and I caught myself on about the seventh note and smeared into 'Listen to the Lambs'"

Fifteen million dollars. Was Wittgenstein's when he died in 1951.

What will suffice? The vice-president of the Hartford Accident & Indemnity Insurance Company had obsessed over.

What to want? Dr. William Williams would ask himself.

Arthur Schopenhauer. Theodore Dreiser. Amy Lowell. Being the diverse influences of Langston Hughes.

Nabokov's ridicule of Faulkner's "corncobby" oeuvre.

The Abyss of Human Illusions

Wondering if the grandson of a Russian gold mine tycoon could have understood the economically depressed, racially charged American South. Or would have deemed it worthwhile to try.

　　　At Lamb House, in Rye, Henry James had no fewer than eight writing desks.
And most often paced back and forth dictating.

Someone once broke into Francis Picabia's flat and stole all his *valuables*. A post-burglary inventory confirmed that no paintings had been taken.

Nabokov's delight at netting (*i.e.* killing) butterflies for his colorful collection.

Smerdyakov was known to torture and kill cats as a boy.

To be fair, Wittgenstein loathed his fortune and did everything he could to unburden himself of it.

On today's pass through this manuscript, Author wondering why he felt the need to further qualify passages as "chapters" or "stanzas" when *passage* is

AFTERWORD, BY DAVID MARKSON, a book by [name of author]

so apt.

Pieces of Sappho's lost work were found cut into strips inside dead Egyptians. Novelist had reminded us.

Dr. Paterson having made note of it decades earlier.

> How easy to slip
> into the old mode, how hard to
> cling firmly to the advance

The Pre-Raphaelites began as a secret society.

Frank Stella and Carl Andre were roommates.

Jackson Pollock laid his canvasses flat on the floor.

The Marquis de Sade was a redhead.

Clem Greenberg refused to give the eulogy at Pollock's funeral, because Jackson had, after all, killed a young woman.

Carl Andre's defense lawyer argued that "hot-blooded" artist Ana Mendieta had committed suicide because of career envy. A motivation not to be found in most suicide prevention pamphlets.

Samuel Beckett's praise for Jules Verne. And Agatha Christie. And Kurt Vonnegut.

The latter having been another good friend of Novelist's.

> Thinking with someone else's brain.
> Schopenhauer called reading.

How much money fifteen and fifty million dollars must have been in 1951 & 1977 respectively.

Frank Sinatra taught Sammy Davis Jr. how to swim.

Except that what I am now thinking about is the person who was next in line, as a pupil of Vermeer. And then the person who was a pupil of the pupil of Vermeer.

Elizabeth Bishop's 15 years in Brazil with Lota de Macedo Soares.

The Book of Disquiet

I can control the flow of paint; there is no accident. Pollock insisted.

A man of genius makes no mistakes. His errors are volitional and are the portals of discovery. Stephen Dedalus asserted.

Flaubert having written the same sort of letter to Victor Hugo.

Researching the net worth of his beloved Modernists, Author discovers that the majority died penniless or obscenely wealthy. And finding more of the latter than the former.

Some affluence, if only half perceived...

What Is to Be Done?

Old. Tired. Sick. Alone. Broke.

...having little or no money in my purse...

AFTERWORD, BY DAVID MARKSON, a book by [name of author]

Joe Gould's *Oral History of Our Time*

Marguerite Young taught at Shortridge High School in Indianapolis. One of her students was Kurt Vonnegut.

Friends die.

Author pretty sure Pollock's declaration was an attempt to maintain the aura of mastery. So people would stop alluding to "a five year old" in their appraisals of his work.

Be careful, lest in casting out your demon you exorcise the best thing in you. William Blake admonished.

Rat Pack lore. Monkees *in memoriam*. A thinly veiled copyright defense of Vanilla Ice.

Which of these things doesn't belong? Sesame Street asked kids.

In a sort of post-structuralist montage interrogating the ontological commitments of identity, text, possession and posterity, how many lines should be devoted to belittling Def Leppard? Author has to ask himself.

The novel perhaps cheapened thereby. Yet giving a damn, Author isn't. Because this is not a novel.

It's whatever the hell Author says it is.

Roland Barthes was a Marxist for a while. But he got bored with it.

James Merrill's father was the co-founder of Merrill Lynch.

THESE LOW TONALITIES!

Dave's not here, man.

The going rate for an indulgence depended on one's station, and ranged from 25 gold florins for kings and queens and archbishops down to three florins for merchants and just one quarter florin for the poorest of believers.

And yet the spirit abides

Dead?

Neither Cheech nor Chong. Septua- and octogenarian respectively.

Scott Moorhead. Jeff Buckley was known as growing up.

Rudolph Kreutzer never performed the Kreutzer Sonata.

If this text were to survive even a decade or two, a later edition would require many asterisks. Because just about everyone still alive as Author now writes will by then be dead.

Author–a distinct possibility–included.

"Goodbye, everybody!"

Timor mortis conturbat me.

Leibniz invented the calculator.

Nick Drake studied English Literature at Cambridge.

AFTERWORD, BY DAVID MARKSON, a book by [name of author]

Author has found a publisher for this manuscript and must now begin the arduous task of substantiating his many unsubstantiated (hearsaid) claims.

Vanilla Ice is 54.

      Wastebasket.

Author has almost immediately decided to leave the text as is and just let people call him on stuff. Because people seem to enjoy that.

Something instead of nothing.

Sir And. What is 'pourquoi'? do or not do?

              And found and lost again and again…

Vonnegut and Novelist had walked the streets of the same borough for many years. The former dying therein, three years before the latter.

Everything was beautiful and nothing hurt.

      Selah.

perhaps only Dr Williams (Bill Carlos)
        will understand its importance
its benediction.
        Ezra Pound had worried.

AFTERWORD, BY DAVID MARKSON, a book by [name of author]

Operator #17, a Lebanese military intelligence officer who was assigned to monitor the Corniche, Beirut's seafront promenade. Instead of videotaping the various political agents, agitators and subversives who gathered there in the evenings, the officer trained his camera on the sunsets over the Mediterranean sea.

More than 16,000. Children of Palestine.

174517–which Primo Levi could read tattooed on his left forearm from Auschwitz onward.

Writing poetry is barbaric. (Afterward.) Adorno declared.

2.5 megacuries. The estimated amount of radioactive gas released into the environment at Three Mile Island.

12 days before the partial meltdown, *The China Syndrome* debuts in movie theaters around the U.S.

Einstein's letter to FDR.

Reports indicate that wildlife is finally returning to the Chernobyl exclusion zone.

Though refused materials such as books, pens, and paper, Wole Soyinka still wrote a significant body of poems and notes criticizing the Nigerian government while in prison.

Just visiting. Was Waldo when Thoreau responded to the former's "What are you doing in here?" with "What are *you* doing *out there*?"

Kant's categorical imperative.

AFTERWORD, BY DAVID MARKSON, a book by [name of author]

Nietzsche's.

Adorno's.

Best wishes and love from
everyone who was here,

Operator #17 was dismissed in 1996 after shooting about a year's worth of sunsets.

So this is the little woman that wrote the book that started this great war?

Marianne Moore wrote the liner notes for Muhammad Ali's spoken word album, *I am the Greatest.*

"...the most glorious of triumphs in the known history of literature." Walt Whitman called *Leaves of Grass* in a pseudonymous review.

It ain't bragging if you can do it. Dizzy Dean insisted.

St. Helena is a small island. Napoleon had written in one of his elementary school notebooks.

Beethoven's 3rd. (Deemed undesirably original.)

Ava Duvernay's *13th.*

3 strikes.

*No Viet Cong ever called me n*****.* Muhammad Ali, under arrest for draft evasion, pointed out.

Amiri Baraka's radical, transgressive, heart-stopping *Dutchman.*
Novelist was also forgetting groundbreaking.

Superpredators. Clinton called them.

Reagan looking at the bright side of the A.I.D.S. epidemic and the war on drugs.

Grenada.

with little to no explanation

America is back!

Oliver North.

hanging chads

Cheney & Rumsfeld

> *America this is quite serious.*

Gore Vidal being related to Al Gore. According to the former, but not the latter.

> *Dead?*

Hollywood Hills. Gore Vidal died in. 2012.

Cousin Al is 74.

Newark, NJ. Amiri Baraka died in. 2014.

Nathan Zuckerman appears in 17 of Philip Roth's novels.

The American Phrenological Journal. Whitman's rave review having appeared in.

> *I greet you at the beginning of a great career, which must have had a long*

AFTERWORD, BY DAVID MARKSON, a book by [name of author]

foreground somewhere, for such a start.

Critics on the right deemed Nelson Mandela a communist terrorist. Those on the far-left found him too eager to reconcile with apartheid supporters.

Robben Island, Pollsmoor Prison and Victor Verster Prison. Being residences claimed by Mandela over a 27 year period of his life.

Abu Ghraib.

Guantanamo.

An Inconvenient Truth. Brought to you by a neoliberal whose ideology is predicated on the willful ignorance thereof.

"...lacking the intelligence of a baboon." Whitman wrote of negroes in one essay. The disconnect from his egalitarian creative work as bizarre and egregious as Heidegger's, though not nearly as contested.

Wole Soyinka is 87. Living in Abeokuta, Nigeria.

a long foreground somewhere

Half of the world's coral reefs have died in the last 30 years.

Remembering the 20 patients and orderlies of the mental hospital who died in the bombing of Grenada. Is anybody?

The Dying Grass

Footage of Operator #17's sunsets was donated to the Atlas Group and can be viewed on their website.

AFTERWORD, BY DAVID MARKSON, a book by [name of author]

The term "social media" was coined in 1997 by an AOL executive.

Mir.   How beauteous mankind is! O brave new world, that has such people in 't!

and the nothing that is

The three most dispiriting words in the English language are Joyce Carol Oates. Gore Vidal declared long before Oates had opened a Twitter account.

Vidal's Burr.

Lin Manuel Miranda's.

China. Egypt. India. Arabia.

Twitter.

& its Discontents

College roommates: Hegel, Hölderlin, and Schelling.

Author had deemed it possible he was the first to appropriate people of the book, but today finds that Michel Leiris preceded him in *Frail Riffs*. (Likely preceded by others.)

The difficulty determining *the first* of something. It being almost as if nothing had ever quite been the first of anything.

Make it new. Had already been old hat by the time Ezra Pound had proclaimed it. Ryan Ruby points out that Jed Rasula had pointed out.

AFTERWORD, BY DAVID MARKSON, a book by [name of author]

Do you know nothing about your beginning? The
H.M.S. Bellipotent's captain asks Billy Budd.

Oates being the literary equivalent of Netflix.
Hundreds of titles and nothing worthwhile.

Kanem. Bachwezi. Great Zimbabwe.

The Greek Myths. As reimagined by Lynn Nottage
and Percival Everett.

> When I sally in on a stallion with the first
> black battalion

The basic fact that we're all more or less Namibian.

Hall & Oates appeared on Soul Train in 1982. And
then again in 1984.

George Orwell named names. (e.g. Charlie Chaplin.)
And coined the term "Cold War".

Sans eyes, sans teeth, sans tears, sans everything.
Marx on Hegel's philosophy.

Jacques. Pronounced Jakes (16th century idiom for
"toilet") or *Jay-queez* depending on the meter and
context in Shakespeare's *As You Like It.*

Fairies and ghosts. Sir Arthur Conan Doyle believed in.

*...in a few thousand years, I who regard you will also
have sprung from the loins of African kings.* Shreve
tells Quentin in the final scene of *Absalom, Absalom!*

433 East 82nd Street. New York apartment building
where Harper Lee may have chit-chatted with
Hall and/or Oates in the hallways of their shared

residence.

In September of 1931, Orwell disguised himself as a tramp and worked as a hop-picker on a farm in West Malling.

J.D. Salinger was a cruise director aboard the MS KUNGSHOLM.

Potato chip inspector. Having been Octavia E. Butler's job title for a time.

Jack London was an oyster pirate.

...to hunt in the morning, fish in the afternoon, rear cattle in the evening...

Kafka was a vegetarian.

(disambiguation)

Kafka is the offensive coordinator for the New York Giants.

Friedrich, did you jot something in the margins of my *Critique of Pure Reason*?
No, Friedrich, I didn't.
...*Wilhelm!*

Today's thirst for knowledge Google: Are Joyce Carol Oates and John Oates related?

...inconclusive.

We do not know everything and we are going to die. Georges Bataille reminded us.

Flatmates in Toronto: Neil Young and Rick James.

AFTERWORD, BY DAVID MARKSON, a book by [name of author]

Who let the coon in? Wallace Stevens reputedly asked as Gwendolyn Brooks entered a National Book Awards banquet.

Modernism. The pretentious self-importance of which Author cannot help giggling about. Despite having cut his literary teeth thereupon and adulating its illustrious dead.

> *Very well then I contradict myself,*
> *(I am large, I contain multitudes.)*

…in the smithy of my soul

(disambiguation)

James Joyce career goals: 1 (but memorable)

Bend it like Beckett.

Wondering what happened to the other seventeen hundred unincinerated pages of *Juneteenth*.

Pentimenti of redacted or rearranged notecards.

Less than 5% of the Universe is visible.

Asterisk #1. Apparently "and well" was inaccurate. RIP Jean-Luc Godard (1930-2022).

> *it's a cold and it's a broken hallelujah*

Beckett on his legendary mentor: *I still think of him as one of the greatest literary geniuses of all time, but I believe I felt very early on that the thing that drew me and the means that I could call on were virtually the opposite of his thing and his means.*

Author perhaps reading what isn't there between the lines to imagine that honorific may have been barbed. For what "greatest literary genius" would have been worth to Joyce's protégé.

He did close with: *I think of him with unqualified admiration, affection, and gratitude.*

Wallace Stevens and T.S. Eliot took as much (if not more) pride in their well-paying bourgeois careers as they did in their poetry.

The last time someone mentioned Wyndham Lewis.

Fifteen minutes of fame. Andy Warhol predicted everyone would have one day.

America Online.

March of 2020. The morning after which Author began to write this book.

Going viral.

Weary of snark and wanting to be a kinder, gentler person, Author takes it back. There are some worthwhile documentaries on Netflix.

Virginia Woolf took up a collection to free Eliot from his day job.

And to be fair, band members of Def Leppard have lived what could reasonably be called a life, which is more than an outside observer could say for whatever it is Author and Reader have been doing all these years.

Terence, this is stupid stuff…

AFTERWORD, BY DAVID MARKSON, a book by [name of author]

Chronicles of Narnia totaling 10.

Fantasy. A literary genre of stuff that is *especially* not really happening.

Eliot politely declined the assistance.

> *When the tongues of flame are in-*
> *folded*
> *Into the crowned knot of fire*
> *And the fire and the rose are one.*

He had never faced fire except at the kitchen range. Delacroix said of Rousseau.

"Something has happened to me at last!" Giacometti exclaimed after being hit by a car while crossing the Place d'Italie.

Jeanette Winterson's adoptive mother was mentally ill.

Dr. Holmes insisting there was nothing wrong with Septimus Smith.

Shortly before Smith's defenestration.

Unica Zürn's.

Ana Mendieta's.

Deleuze's.

The Greatest Man in the World

Holmes is *on* you.

> Good morning, Rembrandt. Good morning to

you, Spinoza. I was extremely sorry to hear about your bankruptcy, Rembrandt. I was extremely sorry to hear about your excommunication, Spinoza.

Davy Jones. David Bowie was known as in the early days. And may have stuck with the birth name if not for the advent of The Monkees. A fact Novelist would not have considered, much less informed the reader of.

But that was then and this is now. Mickey Dolenz sang in The Monkees' comeback anthem of 1989.

> Photography is not Art. Writer on record as having asserted.

Nor were moving pictures. Art. To Writer.

> There is no such thing as a great movie. A Rembrandt is great. Mozart chamber music. Said Marlon Brando. (Notes Novelist.)

Popular music being Art to Writer? One need not wonder.

> *Now I've heard there was a secret chord*
> *That David played, and it pleased the Lord*
> *But you don't really care for music, do you?*

Keith Foti, a roadie in Jeff Buckley's band, had just moved a radio and guitar away from shore, where the tugboat's wake was spilling over the riverbank.

> *I looked up and you were gone.*

Virginia Woolf belittling James Joyce like a duchess dressing down her servants.

Plato's Republic. In which class conflict is posited as

AFTERWORD, BY DAVID MARKSON, a book by [name of author]

inevitable.

For what being Art is worth.

Albert was the only literate member of the Camus family.

Sir John Gielgud turned his nose up at an offer to appear in a performance of *Endgame* in 1958, remarking: I couldn't find anything I liked in the play… it nauseates me.

Neither of Author's parents attended university. (Only one had finished high school.) And Author lived just above the poverty line for about a decade. Which may account for the class-war chip on his shoulder.

Heraclitus. Parmenides had been greatly influenced by.

The Monkees having been a hippie youth phenomenon manufactured by the establishment. Capitalized (bubble-gumized) counter-culture. Until they defiantly crashed and burned at the height of their fame with the drug-addled, psychedelic travesty, Head, written by Jack Nicholson and directed by Bob Rafelson.

The latter having died a few weeks ago.

Jack Nicholson, who starred in Rafelson's follow-up project, *Five Easy Pieces*, is 85.

Wotton Underwood, U.K. Sir John Gielgud died in. May of 2000. Days after being directed by Harold Pinter in *Catastrophe* for the Beckett on Film project.

In which Gielgud plays a statue with no lines.

Ch-ch-ch-changes…
David Bowie (*né* Jones) sang the ineluctable nature of.

Panta Rhei. (All is flux.) Heraclitus may well have believed, but never stated as such.

London. Harold Pinter died in. 2008.

Nobody comes. Nobody calls.

No word was ever as effective as a rightly timed pause. Mark Twain observed.

That cretinous Frank Sinatra film. Writer referred to the film version of *Dingus Magee* as.

Las Manos de Orlac. Con Peter Lorre. The movie poster of which is repeatedly sighted in *Under the Volcano*.

Rodin's secretary. Rilke had been.

Molly Bloom's monologue.

…for the growing good of the world…

Operator #17.

Then again, quoting himself or not, Novelist naturally does receive some few phone calls after all.
All too often in these years with news of someone's death, however.

Los Angeles. Sinatra and Brando both died in. 1998 and 2004 respectively.

My second-best bed. The Bard bequeathed his

AFTERWORD, BY DAVID MARKSON, a book by [name of author]

widow.

> *A dim and silent shedful of your life's*
> *supplies*
> *When all you need's a coffin and your*
> *Sunday best*
> *To smarten up the end.*
> > Frightened Rabbit front man
> > Scott Hutchison sang in *Things*.

Unamuno's *Tragic Sense of Life*.

Scott's mam called him the frightened rabbit
because of his chronic shyness.

Emily Dickinson was believed to have severe social
anxiety. Hence her not leaving the house for years.

The Plague.

And her practice of entertaining guests from an
adjacent room.

When the Camus family attended the cinema, Arthur
had to read the title cards aloud. Which mortified
him.

Mother died today.

The above is not, alas, a sequent literary allusion; it is
Author stating a fact.

Jesus wept. Being the shortest verse in the bible.
Recited at a church service in *Juneteenth*, by a boy
who had forgotten the verse he was meant to have
memorized.

Spinoza was known to sometimes go as long

as three full months without once stepping out of doors.

If I live, I will go to Amherst–if I die, I certainly will. Benjamin Newton wrote Emily Dickinson. And may have been dead by the time the letter arrived.

> *Let me know if you are going.*

Knight of the Rueful (/Mournful) Countenance.

Coleridge composed *The Rime of the Ancient Mariner* in Shropshire.

Is it difficult to speak? Author had asked his mother in the waning hours, as he was able to
understand little of her constant murmuring.
Terribly difficult to speak. Was her anomalously lucid response.
Then don't try to speak, just rest. Author advised.
That's even harder. Being more or less the last coherent thing she said to Author.

My earliest friend. Emily referred to Ben Newton as.

> *And I couldn't awake from the nightmare*
> *that sucked me in and pulled me under*
> Jeff Buckley sang.

In the song, *So Real*.

A Shropshire Lad. Housman had not been. Born and raised in Worcestershire.

> *White in the moon the long road lies*
> *That leads me from my love*

AFTERWORD, BY DAVID MARKSON, a book by [name of author]

Go Down, Moses

From atop the minaret. The muezzin would call muslims to prayer. Before the advent of loudspeakers.

el Caballero de la triste figura

Gentlemen, it is five o'clock. Class is over. Henri Bergson's last words following a suddenly lucid lecture from his deathbed.

Author not knowing how to feel or what to do today. Goes on Authoring.

Housemates at 46 Gordon Square in Bloomsbury: Virginia Woolf and John Maynard Keynes.

Sweny's Lemon Soap. Plumtree's Potted Meat.

I publish these poems, few though they are, because it is not likely that I shall ever be impelled to write much more.

I looked up and you were gone.

Scottish band Frightened Rabbit saw brief commercial success in the U.S. with *Swim Until You Can't See Land* which was featured on the soundtrack of Jodie Foster's *The Beaver*, starring Mel Gibson.

John Hinckley Jr.

Taxi Driver

That's right. *Nine*.

Holden Caulfield.

Chapman's Homer.

Snark-weary Author wanting to forgive Mel Gibson because he recalls him seeming genuinely ashamed and remorseful after the DUI rant and the quality of mercy is in short supply these days.

> *(Just like) Starting Over*

Author having unintentionally quoted an anti-Semitic play and then followed it with a domestic abuser allusion in his defense of Gibson (himself guilty of etc.). But almost immediately recognizing this faux pas.

A moment too late, Author fears.

Yet still wanting to forgive. To leave open the possibility of growth.

> *You must change your life.*

John Lennon owning up to his violent tendencies. For what that may have been worth.

Brahms was abused as a child. As were George Orwell and Lord Byron.

> *Als ich kahn.*

Author's sweeping dismissal of JCO's oeuvre despite having only read three of her books (and quite liking one of them) for the sake of a zinger. Being a sorry sign of the times.

> *What thou lovest well remains*
> *the rest is dross*
> *What thou lov'st well shall not be reft*

AFTERWORD, BY DAVID MARKSON, a book by [name of author]

from thee
What thou lov'st well is thy true heritage
how mean thy hates
Fostered in falsity,
pull down thy vanity,
Rathe to destroy, niggard in charity...

Why do you hate the South? Shreve asks Quentin in the closing scene of *Absalom, Absalom!*

In the naval town of Portsmouth, England in 1761, Mason & Dixon meet for the first time. After brief discussions of their respective background, the two retire to an ale house for libations before their departure on the frigate HMS Seahorse to observe the Transit of Venus from Sumatra as ordered by the Royal Society.

That's not life for men and women, insult and hatred. And everybody knows that it's the very opposite of that...Love...I mean the opposite of hatred. Bloom informs *the citizen.*

I don't hate it...I don't. I don't! I don't hate it! I don't hate it! Quentin insists.

Queen. The lady doth protest too much, methinks.

I put the rose in my hair like the Andalusian girls...

In Yoko Ono's *Ceiling Painting* of 1966, the London gallery-goer (John Lennon having been one such) had to climb a ladder and hold a magnifying glass up to a tiny word painted on the ceiling.

Yes. Having been the word.

I am undertaking a 60-kilometre bicycle ride. Either I shall not get there or I shall not get back. But I shall set out, weather permitting. Samuel Beckett informs a correspondent.

Hesiod's *Works and Days*. 700 B.C.

Alluded to in *The Lovesong of J. Alfred Prufrock*. Around a million days later.

> *Since then 'tis centuries;*
> *But each*
> *Feels shorter than the day*

Sun Day. Moon Day.

Tyr's Day. Woden's Day.

Thor's Day. Freya Day.

Saturn Day.

Happy Days.

Samuel Beckett risked his life for the French Resistance in WWII. And would live to see the Berlin Wall fall in 1989. Dying shortly thereafter. In Paris. On a Freya Day.

TGIF

Farewell and be kind.

That is what I find so wonderful, that not a day goes by....hardly a day, without some addition to one's knowledge however trifling, the addition I mean, provided one takes the pains. Winnie muses in *Happy Days.*

And goes on to reflect: *Sometimes all is over, for the day, all done, all said, all ready for the night, and the day not over, far from over, the night not ready, far, far from ready.*

AFTERWORD, BY DAVID MARKSON, a book by [name of author]

Beethoven's Tenth.

Author's Fifth.

> *He knew he could have started a third book on the day he posted the second. He knew also that the third would be blood sibling in kind and quality to the earlier two, as would a tenth to the third.*
>> A peripheral character concedes in Novelist's first "serious" novel.

Vaya Usted con Dios...y que no haya novedad.

The above from *The Recognitions*, not *Under the Volcano*. Most of the unindented, unattributed quotes herein being from one or the other.

> ...a cult did form

It's not the copy. It's the signature.

Arthur Rimbaud. Harper Lee. Paul Valéry. Ferdinand de Saussure. Louis-René des Forêts

> Writer is pretty much tempted to quit writing.

Literary aspirations incompletely stifled. Reads the dossier of the jumper from Beckett's *Rough for Theatre II*.

Strindberg's *Inferno Crisis*

Robert Musil suffered long bouts of writer's block. He would throw a blanket over his desk and walk round and round it, smoking, for days.

> ...that character in *The Plague*, Joseph

Grand....Who rewrites the same opening sentence for a novel eternally, with only minimal variations....

Le Mythe de Sisyphe

There is only one really philosophical problem.

Vita Sackville-West. Virginia Woolf had based *Orlando* on.

> *I think I'll save suicide for another year.* Scott Hutchison sang in *Floating in the Forth* (2008).

Knowing what comes next in Shakespeare.

Spoiler alert: Malone Dies.

>   *Dead?*

Nick Drake overdosed on antidepressants in 1974.

I expect to die at the age of 85. Edouard Levé's gross miscalculation.

...a great-hearted man has killed himself...for the sake of an idea, for the sake of Hecuba...Dostoevsky's *Raw Youth* exclaims.

Southey and Coleridge were roommates in Bristol.

The age of 15 is the middle of my life, regardless of when I die. Levé more accurately intuited.

But I shall set out, weather permitting...

If it had been some other word painted on the ceiling, *who knows*...John Lennon tells Dick Cavett.

AFTERWORD, BY DAVID MARKSON, a book by [name of author]

Maybe we're fished for.

…and then I asked him with my eyes to ask again…

Remember, Dear, an unfaltering yes is my only reply to your utmost question–Emily assures Sue.

Whole Lotta Love

And I let the fish go.

Tea's on, Bob. Shall I be mother?

Hitchcock had his secretary buy up all the known copies of Robert Bloch's novel to try and keep the twist ending of *Psycho* concealed.

"Gorky was copying Picasso. Pollock was copying Picasso. De Kooning was copying Picasso."

Motherwell?

Then don't try to speak, just rest.

Jump the shark refers to the moment a series has lost its narrative momentum and is now just clowning around.

Coined in 1985, referring to The Fonz's waterskiing exploits on the 50s nostalgia sit-com (airing in the 70s & 80s) *Happy Days*.

Mike Nesmith and Mickey Dolenz had both auditioned to be The Fonz.

The Monkees are more like the Marx Brothers than the Fab Four. Said John Lennon.

Groucho. Harpo. Chico. Gummo. Zeppo.

Karl. (No relation.)

Touchstone. Costard. Puck. Falstaff. Feste.

> Youth's a stuff will not endure

Lear's fool. Unnamed.

King. I know thee not, old man.

The Player King.

What's Hecuba to him or he to Hecuba?

> that is the question

South Queensferry, Scotland. Where Scott Hutchison committed suicide in 2018.

The Awful Rowing Toward God. Anne Sexton insisted not be published until after her death.

Nevermore of peace. Will Quentin have.

> Reader has come to this place because he had no life back there at all.

AFTERWORD, BY DAVID MARKSON, a book by [name of author]

Hart Crane. Archibald MacLeish. John Berryman. Robert Bly. Amy Clampitt. Carl Sandburg. William Stafford.

Among those who've written poems about Emily Dickinson.

William Luce, Eloïse Heger-Hedløy & Susan Glaspell each wrote a play about her.

An entire genre of fictions, essays and bios about her. (Author has authored two. Three if you count this one.)

People of the book.

A Buddhist Jew with attachments to Krishna, Siva, Allah, Coyote and the Sacred Heart. Allen Ginsberg described his religious affiliation.

> *Some keep the Sabbath going to church–*
> *I keep it staying at home–*

Ginsberg singing William Blake's *The Garden of Love*.

Encore, Billie Holiday, *encore*!

Black, lesbian, mother, warrior, poet. Audre Lorde self-described.

Mahogany. Joe Sedley's father worries Joe's mixed race children (with prospective bride, Miss Swartz) might turn out in *Vanity Fair*.

A Collection of Unpublished Letters of William Makepeace Thackeray. Published posthumously by Charles Scribner's Sons, 1887.

AFTERWORD, BY DAVID MARKSON, a book by [name of author]

Beckett's *Dream of Fair to Middling Women* reads like James Joyce juvenilia.

As does Novelist's 2nd "serious" novel.

As do thousands of others written in the last century. (Many of them worthwhile all the same.)

A Rose for Emily. By ~~Edgar Allan Poe~~ William Faulkner.

undesirable originality

Beckett's Belacqua.

Dante's.

       Do you know where you're going to?

My father was a mulatto, my grandfather was a Negro, and my great-grandfather was a monkey. As you can see sir, my family starts where ends yours. Alexandre Dumas responded to one of the many racial epithets hurled at him.

Bias. Heraclitus and many others have been greatly influenced by.

Bias of Priene, that is.

      This is my page for English B.

Jackie Robinson was a Republican. As was Zora Neale Hurston.

Karl Marx died at his desk.

The Beirut correspondent for NPR's *All Things Considered*. Carolyn Forche had been.

The beach, or the cemetery?

What follows for Protagonist in either case?

Vladimir Mayakovsky: a Tragedy. By Vladimir Mayakovsky.

Jack London may or may not have committed suicide.

Haruki Murakami's first novel, *Hear the Wind Sing* was inspired by a "personal epiphany" he'd had at a Tokyo Yakult Swallows baseball game.

...if that is in any way connected to anything?

To Build a Fire. Author recalls greatly disliking when he read it at Robert Frost Junior High School, because it had vicariously distressed him and made him feel cold. (Born and raised in Chicago, he had a *mind of winter.*)

The minor miracle of which only recognized in retrospect as the turning point of his life.

Out of the Cradle Endlessly Rocking

...my whole body so cold no fire could warm me

You are in love, Mr. Stoner. It is as simple as that.

I was a Flower of the mountain yes

Aime-je un rêve?

In her paper sculptures, Lesley Dill uses a blend of exotic papers, including rice and metallic papers, to

AFTERWORD, BY DAVID MARKSON, a book by [name of author]

fashion dresses and necklaces reminiscent of Emily Dickinson's customary attire; she then lithographs Dickinson's text onto the sculptures.

Leon.　　*What fine chisel*
　　　　　Could ever yet cut breath?
　　　　　Let no man mock me,
　　　　　For I will kiss her!

　　　　Anybody can be nobody. Said Eugene V. Debs.

James Joyce's eye patch affectation.

As well him as another. Molly Bloom recalls thinking.

I am no man. Ulysses tells the Cyclops.

–A new apostle to the gentiles…Universal love. The citizen wryly responds to Bloom's affirmation.

Conrad Aiken enumerating poets in the anthology he's editing: *Emily Dickinson (the only dead one invited), Amy Lowell, Edgar Lee Masters…*

Harvard of the Spoon River Valley. Author refers to his alma mater as.

Thoreau having written the same sort of letter to Emerson.

Italo Svevo was the model for Leopold Bloom?

beauty added to strangeness

This especially cruel April, two more progenitors have passed. *Adieu* John Barth & Paul Auster.

That life begins and ends is man's conception, not nature's. Quoth Auster.

Samuel Barber. Aaron Copland. Jan Meyerowitz. Vincent Persichetti. Rudolf Escher.

Each set Emily Dickinson's poetry to music.

> *Now in a moment I know what I am for, I awake,*
>
> *And already a thousand singers, a thousand songs, clearer, louder and more sorrowful than yours, A thousand warbling echoes have started to life within me, never to die.*

Granted, Reader is essentially the I in instances such as that.

The mind/body problem still being a problem. Despite the many theorists who claim to have solved or dissolved it.

Consciousness Explained. By Daniel Dennett.

Mission Accomplished!

Technology's drive to render all things one thing. Or zero things.

Seven Types of Ambiguity

How to Read and Why. By Harold Bloom.

Right You Are (if you think so)

Luigi Pirandello donated his Nobel Prize to the Fascist

AFTERWORD, BY DAVID MARKSON, a book by [name of author]

government for their "Gold to the Fatherland" campaign during the Second Italo-Ethiopian War.

> *Emerging from an Abyss, and reentering it–that is Life, is it not, Dear?*

Goodbye everybody!

Falling out of Nabokov and Edmund Wilson. Over diction.

Falling out of Colin McGinn and Michael Dummett. Over syntax.

How Jeff Buckley becomes a character in this "novel" by virtue of ambiguation.

> *jamais n'abolira le hasard*

The way things continue to happen while one is writing a book. Coincident with the "plot" of whatever Author is Authoring.

Reelection.

Rafah.

Terribly difficult to speak.

Conrad Aiken's father shot his mother. And then himself.

Dream Songs

No doubt you are a flawed and wounded person who's carried a wound in him from the very beginning. Why else would you have spent the whole of your adult life bleeding words onto a page? Paul

Auster answers and asks himself in *The Winter Journal*.

> *It was snowing*
> *And it was going to snow.*

The Washington Avenue Bridge. In Minneapolis.

You will be cold. You are cold now. Bon informs Henry in *Absalom, Absalom!*.

Sylvia Plath's *Daddy* is about her mother?

Laura Ingalls Wilder refused to say "obey" in her wedding vows.

Michael Landon's mother was mentally ill.

"commiserate"

Freud's pupil. H.D. called herself.

kaleidoscope gifted with consciousness

> Where will protagonist have been born?

...though ill from paralysis, [Whitman] consented to hobble up and silently take a seat on the platform, but refused to make any speech, saying, "I have felt a strong impulse to come over and be here today myself in memory of Poe, which I have obeyed; but not the slightest impulse to make a speech, which, my dear friends, must also be obeyed."

Letter to the World. The Emily Dickinson bio-dance performed by Martha Graham. Barbara Morgan's photograph of the performance captures Graham kicking her leg over her back, with her white dress swept up about her.

AFTERWORD, BY DAVID MARKSON, a book by [name of author]

...have started to life within me, never to die

AFTERWORD, BY DAVID MARKSON, a book by [name of author]

Lou Reed playing someone who looks like Lou Reed in a demo reel Harvey Keitel and Mira Sorvino watch in the Paul Auster film, *Lulu on the Bridge*.

Hart Crane. John Berryman had been greatly influenced by.

So long, everybody! Having been Alex Trebek's sign-off for Jeopardy.

Tchaikovsky had expressed a fear of literally losing his head.

As had David Foster Wallace.

Let them eat brioche. Was what Marie Antoinette had purportedly said, though it is unlikely she'd said anything of the sort.

Rimbaud lost his right leg after a misdiagnosis deemed it necessary to amputate.

My bad. An expression first used by Louis Armstrong on the Ed Sullivan show.

It's all good. Blake, Whitman, and Rilke insisted.

This poet died in Haiku.

Who is W.S. Merwin?

Swinburne and Dante Gabriel Rossetti lived together at 16 Cheyne Walk in Chelsea.

Andy Kaufman playing a record of the Mighty Mouse theme song and lip-syncing to its refrain.

Pessoa helped Aleister Crowley fake his own death.

AFTERWORD, BY DAVID MARKSON, a book by [name of author]

The Mountain Eagle. Hitchcock's second film. Of which no prints exist.

Allen Ginsberg's mother was mentally ill.

Sarah Bernhardt also lost a leg. As did Mikhail Bakhtin.

Frida Kahlo considered her prosthetic leg a work of art.

About 50% of the artwork in circulation is fake. According to a 2014 report by the Switzerland Fine Arts Expert Institute.

Corot painted 2,000 canvases, 5,000 of which are in America. ARTnews reported in 1953.

Blaise Cendrars lost an arm. As did Paul Wittgenstein, C.S. Giscombe, Ramón María del Valle-Inclán, and Def Leppard's drummer, Rick Allen.

The phantom limb in William Dean Howells' *Editha.*

Operator #17.

About a century after his death, fans of Galileo removed three fingers, a tooth, and a vertebra from his mausoleum for souvenirs.

Robert Creeley lost an eye. Van Gogh "lost" an ear. Tycho Brahe lost a nose.

Gogol claimed that "evil spirits" had forced him to burn the second volume of *Dead Souls.*

Frankenstein. Mary Shelley dreamed up to entertain Byron & Bysshe on a rainy afternoon.

Someone will have to piece me together. Don Delillo quoting Jack Ruby in *Libra*.

The spiritual yearning behind the biting satire in *The Recognitions*. Which the author puts away like a childish thing for the remainder of his cynical oeuvre.

The Church at Auvers.

Odds the Kandinsky you're looking at is a Kandinsky: 50/50.

Sosumi. The make of Oscar Crease's car. Which he runs himself over with in Gaddis' litigation satire, *A Frolic of His Own*.

Bleak House

Next Monday Mr. Emerson reads & then at 3 ½ P.M. there is a meeting of the Woman's Club at 3 Tremont Place. Higginson extending an invitation to Emily in one of his letters.

Andy Kaufman reading *The Great Gatsby* to audience groans until finally relenting and playing the record they'd been clamoring for. Which turns out to be a recording of Andy Kaufman reading *The Great Gatsby* from where he'd left off.

Mirrors dominate people. They tell your face how to grow. Esme's explanation for not having one in her apartment (to vain Otto's chagrin) in *The Recognitions*.

City of Glass

& the Wardrobe

AFTERWORD, BY DAVID MARKSON, a book by [name of author]

Lewis Carroll's perhaps not quite healthy preoccupation with his friend's daughter.

Darger's Vivian Girls

> *Here I come to save the day!*
> *Mighty Mouse is on his way!*

Otto's sling and other affectations rehearsed in *The Recognitions*.

...They all talk about painting. Now remember, no matter what anyone says, you just comment on the solids in Uccello. You can say you don't like them, or say they're divine. Can you remember that? The *solids* in Oochello...

Who and/or what Shakespeare is actually savaging in *The Merchant of Venice*.

"A merchant," Stephen said, "is one who buys cheap and sells dear...jew or gentile, is he not?"

Mer.   a plague o' both your houses!

> *Do I contradict myself?*

Sosumi.

The custom of covering mirrors in the home of someone who has died.

> *Knock the glass out! My God—glass, my*
> *townspeople! For what purpose! Is it for*
> *the dead to look out...?*

Novelist's affectations.

Author's.

Jessica Shylock. Being the only character in the play who isn't a shallow, manipulative, self-serving bigot.

Izzy (Harvey Keitel): Hey, that's Lou Reed.
Celia (Mira Sorvino): No, it just looks like him.

Be you! Author will hear Peter Falk exclaim in his mind's ear now and again, apropos of nothing. While admittedly unsure if Falk ever actually says this verbatim in the film or Author is conflating it with something he'd once said to his own mother. And unable to fact-check, because he couldn't get through a re-viewing.

Rudyard Kipling was tortured by his caregivers as a child.

Sartre never knew his father. Ditto Camus.

John Lennon barely knew his.

Robert Graves' son, Mallorca, was tutored by W.S. Merwin.

Author recalling the childhood practice of hurling himself against the back wall of the closet in an attempt to cross the threshold of reality and burst into a land of make-believe. To escape the chronic angers and insanity of his home.

WWQD?

The Locked Room.

It is necessary to assert that basins ought to be and are helmets and to get up a fight about it like the

AFTERWORD, BY DAVID MARKSON, a book by [name of author]

fight they got up at the inn. Unamuno insisted.

For years Author had done this. Over and over and over. Believing he just needed to believe hard enough to break through.

Inquiring after the reception of *Les Miserables*, Victor Hugo sent a sheet of paper with a question mark on it to his publisher.

The response was an exclamation point.

Nabokov invented emoticons.

Author having at some point, in some sense, broken through? Having believed hard enough?

Lost in the Funhouse

Herman Hesse had undergone an exorcism as a child.

As had Jeanette Winterson.

To comfort a little girl who had lost her doll, Kafka wrote letters to her signed by the lost doll.

I'm a Believer. The last song The Monkees performed as a foursome in 2002.

Ibsen's grandfather died at sea. Days after Ibsen's father was born.

Ghosts.

Blake on Milton on Satan.

The increasingly autocratic and eventually beheaded King of England, Charles I.

Milton's thrust unintentional, intentional, semi-intentional?

The only paradise is a paradise lost.

In Search of Lost Time.

Derek Walcott trained as a painter.

Remedios Varo and Leonora Carrington were roommates in Mexico City.

Sharing of premises. Elizabeth Hardwick called cohabitation with Robert Lowell.

"Buonarroti" was one of Hölderlin's pseudonyms in his years of madness in the tower.

In the early days of Michelangelo's career he conspired with de Medici to pass off one of his sculptures as a Greek relic.

Leonardo, Ad Reinhardt, and Sir Isaac Newton dismissed sculpture as an art form.

Stone dolls. Newton called them.

Judge Otis Phillips Lord (and *Master?*)

Lifelong celibacy. Newton cited as his greatest accomplishment.

No word of where this arguable accomplishment

ranked for DesCartes, Spinoza, Kant, Kierkegaard, Wittgenstein, Thoreau, *et al.*

The mortal hatred of the sexes. Nietzsche called it.

Several editors accusing Otto of plagiarism without being able to identify the author he had plagiarized in *The Recognitions.*

Nietzsche attended a performance of Bizet's Carmen more than 20 times.

Deducing the laws of gravity? Calculus? *Nope.*

Advice to the bride. Leibniz would offer as a wedding gift.

Bias was one of the Seven Sages of Greece.

Rimbaud and Verlaine.

Van Gogh and Gauguin.

The best of all possible worlds.

& Punishment

...in the name of what God or what ideal, do you forbid me to live according to my nature? Andre Gide asked society.

If there wasn't death, I think you couldn't go on. Stevie Smith speculated.

I am not a strong swimmer. Stephen Dedalus reminds himself on Sandymount Strand.

The Fall

One did survive the wreck.

Vio.   *Prove true, imagination, O, prove true, That I,*
        dear brother, be now ta'en for you!

Though I never saw him, or had any personal
communication with him, now that he is suddenly
dead I realize that he was nearer, dearer, and more
important to me than anyone else.
Said Tolstoy of Dostoevsky.

Parallel Lives.

Napoleon's leg twitched. Being all the Consul can
recall from *War & Peace.*

Fabrizio del Dongo.

Your illusions are a part of you like your bones and
flesh and memory. Faulkner insisted.

Author prefers to think of this as practicing Novelist's
innovated form. The way one would write a
Petrarchan sonnet, Sapphic lyric or detective story
(Poe™).

For the great fun of it, if nothing else. (Author having
so missed his *Playmate.*)

I read Édouard Levé's Autoportrait and found I
admire its approach to biography. It is an approach
that does not raise one fact above another but lets
the facts stand together in a fruitless clump, like a
life. He wrote it in his 39th year. In my 39th year, this
book follows his. Jesse Ball introducing his variation on
~~Édouard Levé's~~ Joe Brainard's innovated form.

Arnaut Daniel invented the sestina.

AFTERWORD, BY DAVID MARKSON, a book by [name of
author]

Ezra Pound Among the Troubadours

> Voltaire on opera: Anything that is too stupid to be spoken is sung.

Ralph Ellison trained as a musician.

Burning Down the House

Spadework for a Palace. In which Krasznahorkai's protagonist follows Malcolm Lowry's "wavering footsteps". Which had, in turn, been following Melville's.

or the Ambiguities

Method of this work: literary montage. I have nothing to say, only to show…Walter Benjamin on *Passagen-Werk.*

Bildow stripping then tossing all his clothes off the train (disposing of the evidence) so he can wear his new Italian suit home and avoid paying duty at the Swiss border. In *The Recognitions.* Then opening the box and realizing it's a little boy's sailor suit.

Rimbaud in Abyssinia.

> *I was much further out than you thought*

The friendship of Elizabeth Bishop and Derek Walcott.

St. Anne's Episcopal Church in Brooklyn Heights. Where Jeff Buckley made his singing debut. At a memorial concert for his father, the folk icon, Tim Buckley. A man Jeff barely knew.

Every Grass. Emily Dickinson once refers to.

You spoke of Mr. Whitman—I never read his Book—but was told he is disgraceful. Emily writes Higginson.

Which would more likely have been a lure than a deterrent, and so Author considers this remark proof that she *had* in fact read Whitman.

A writer could suspend their soul in language, making the souls of writers like droplets of oil, suspended in the sea of life. Proclaims the protagonist of Sheila Heti's *Pure Colour*.

–Léger, I mean Chagall...
–The emptiness it shows, it hurts to look at. It's so real, so *real*.

At the memorial concert, Buckley covered his father's song, *I Never Asked to Be Your Mountain*.

Then he opened the box from the tailor in Rome. All it contained was a sailor suit made for a boy of seven, with short pants. Nonetheless the hand stitching was fine, the double seams drawn with exquisite care. There was even a little round hat with ribbons, and the name of the first Italian dreadnought, *Dante Alighieri*, embroidered in gold round the band.

ABANDON ALL HOPE, YE WHO ENTER HERE

The Voyage that Never Ends

Kerouac typed *On the Road* onto one continuous scroll of paper.

(Part of which would be eaten by a friend's dog.)

Allen Ginsberg having written the same sort of letter to William Carlos Williams. Which the latter included in *Paterson*.

Something else, something else the same.

Memory Babe. Was Kerouac's nickname growing up.

AFTERWORD, BY DAVID MARKSON, a book by [name of author]

...It's not even past.

I AM THINKING OF YOU.

Love,

Ingeborg

A charter member of the Utopian agricultural collective, Brook Farm. Ha(w)thorne had been.

William Burroughs took the minutes at the Naropa University faculty meetings.

> I am still feeling the typewriter, naturally. And hearing the keys.

Gd crs as mch fr mmnt as fr hr—what mean? Otto puzzling over a notesheet he'd scribbled to himself in *The Recognitions.*

> *Dead?*

Mr. Bowles was not willing to die. Emily informs Higginson.

That's even harder.

> *...I worked later on the Associated Press as a copyboy, and spent most of the last year in a mental hospital; and now I am back in Paterson which is home for the first time in seven years. What I'll do there I don't know yet...*

Ginsberg's unrequited love for Neal Cassady.

The friendship of Edward Thomas and Robert Frost.

Because I liked you better
Than suits a man to say,
It irked you, and I promised
To throw the thought away.
Housman had vowed to
Moses Jackson.

Kerouac having had a brief romance with Gore Vidal.

You're still in your black shoes! With a red dress! Go upstairs quickly and put on your red shoes!

We do not know everything and we are going to die.

"in little autumnal gusts"

Ezra Pound having written the same sort of letter to Thomas Hardy.

Best wishes and love from
everyone who was here,

Jane Austen rejected the farce of matrimony, lived a spinster's life and wrote six novels which all end with weddings.

George Eliot defied society and lived (in sin) the life she damn well pleased. And wrote depressing novels about the crushing weight of ignorance.

she will be near, but unseen...

If first you read my eyes:
Each one is titled
"I'm drowning back to you"
Jeff Buckley sang at the
memorial for his estranged

AFTERWORD, BY DAVID MARKSON, a book by [name of author]

father.

Between the Acts. Published posthumously by the author's widower.

What *The Recognitions* is about. After a close re-reading, Author is not so sure he knew nor now knows.

"Sweetie Pie"

Teaching at a village elementary school in Haidbauer, Wittgenstein was reportedly seen as a tyrant by the slower students, boxing ears and pulling hair. Once even knocking a student unconscious.

I shall look as if I were dead; and that will not be true. The Little Prince foretold.

124 Bluestone Road. In *Beloved*.

We are here! We are here! We are here! The inhabitants of Whoville cry out.

Thoreau studied to be a teacher, but only lasted a few months in the profession. He was dismissed for refusing to administer corporal punishment.

In the Evergreen Cemetery in Stonington, James Merrill and David Jackson are buried side by side.
> WE'VE TIME LEFT ONLY FOR LAST WORDS
> WHAT WILL IT
> BE? SHALL WE DEFY THEM? TURN THE
> CLOCK BACK?

Robert Duncan on H.D.: I have taken psychic being, taken fire from these works. Over years, I have confused myself with them...

Last in a long line of literary kleptomaniacs. Sarah Kane considered herself.

> *I know this letter finds you in good health, as I saw you speak at the museum in N.Y. this week. I ran backstage to accost you, but changed my mind, after waving at you, and ran off again.*
>
> *Respectfully yours,*
>
> *A.G.*

You were not aware that you saved my life.

Beckett outlived Joyce by nearly half a century.

The Voyage that Never Ends

Ellison referring to it as his "novel-in-progress" as far back as 1951.

I think of him with unqualified admiration, affection, and gratitude.

& her mind is said to be perfectly wonderful

She glided in, in white, bearing a Daphne odora for me, & said under her breath..."How long are you going to stay?"

> *–Truly no flower yet withers in your hand.*

"Goodbye, everybody!"

The cruelest month. Allen Ginsberg died in. 1997.

AFTERWORD, BY DAVID MARKSON, a book by [name of author]

Well. For now, I'm dead. We'll see if I can be born again. For now, I'm dead. I'm speaking from my tomb. Clarice Lispector declared in a TV interview.

...but what the hell does it mean?

It all depends on this: *with whom we confuse ourselves.* Elias Canetti maintained.

Was it me? Are you still here? Bliss asks Daddy Hickman from his deathbed in *Juneteenth*.

My dear defrauded longsuffering Malc–

Does nobody understand?

Still, you see, I try.

> Ignore all my nonsense. Just remember my love.
>   Sam

As a boy, Tennyson could recite all 103 of Horace's Odes from memory.

...have started to life within me...

I must go in; the fog is rising...

The last Afternoon that my father lived, therewith no premonition–I preferred to be with him, invented an absence for mother, Vinnie being asleep. He seemed peculiarly pleased as I oftenest stayed with myself, and remarked as the Afternoon withdrew, he "would like it to not end."

Whole Lotta Love

jamais n'abolira le hasard

Dead?

AFTERWORD, BY DAVID MARKSON, a book by [name of author]

Somebody is still living on this beach.

AFTERWORD, BY DAVID MARKSON, a book by [name of author]